Mrs. Alfred Hunt

That Other Person

Vol. 2

Mrs. Alfred Hunt

That Other Person
Vol. 2

ISBN/EAN: 9783337053253

Printed in Europe, USA, Canada, Australia, Japan

Cover: Foto ©Andreas Hilbeck / pixelio.de

More available books at **www.hansebooks.com**

THAT OTHER PERSON

A Novel

BY

MRS ALFRED HUNT

AUTHOR OF 'THORNICROFT'S MODEL' 'THE LEADEN CASKET' ETC.

IN THREE VOLUMES

VOL. II.

London

CHATTO & WINDUS, PICCADILLY

1886

[The right of translation is reserved]

CONTENTS

OF

THE SECOND VOLUME.

THAT OTHER PERSON

CHAPTER XIII.

THE HEART'S MISGIVINGS.

> *Henry.*   Let it content you now,
> There is no woman that I love so well.
> *Ros.*   No woman but should be content with that.
> TENNYSON.

ALL through the bitter month of March there had been days when Josephine Treherne could not refrain from betaking herself to her room and her seat on the old black box, to bewail Mr. Daylesford's forgetfulness of herself and family. He was the only human being who had ever shown any disposition to make their lives happier, and he had ceased to care for them. But Josephine Treherne was not the only girl who was unhappy about Mr. Daylesford. There was one who lived under his own roof who was making herself miserable on much more substantial grounds, and when April came and he sometimes spent many hours of each day in Lorne Gardens, she was still more wretched, though she only partly guessed at where he had been. They had come to England together in November, to a house in Ambassadors' Gate, which Mr. Blackmore had made ready for his client, and then she who had lived with him abroad for nearly four years, and had never been parted from him for more than an hour or so except when he had to go back to England for the trial, suddenly found herself separated from him at every turn, by engagements of various kinds, social conventions, and arrangements, of which she, an inexperienced country girl, had formed no previous conception. She had left her home for his sake, but she had left it to go abroad, and though she knew that she was doing wrong, she was not made to feel it by the visible condemnation of her fellow-crea-tures until she returned to her native land.

She had borne Daylesford's name, and they had for the most part lived in unfrequented places on the Continent, where English travellers were rare. They had avoided every one, and had spent their whole time in sketching. It was a passion with both of them, and those among whom they sojourned willingly left them to themselves.

At length Daylesford had wished to return to his own country; he had his brother's property to look after, and in many respects it was inconvenient for him to be absent. Even when he first came to England, ignorant though he was of English society and its *convenances*, he had felt that he and Hester must no longer reside under the same roof. He had told her that he should seek a pretty home for her in the neighbourhood of London, where he could easily see her without offending that inexorable power called Society.

Hester's ignorance of that power was profound. 'We know no one,' she had said; 'we want to know no one.'

'That cannot last long,' he had replied, and had tried to make her see the thing as he did.

She had, of course, yielded, but she had yielded as people do to the surgeon's knife; and he, while assuring her that this partial separation really must take place, had been so touched by her distress, that he had day after day delayed to make the final arrangements, until February came, and she was still with him.

These months in England had taught her many bitter things, which she might have known before, but somehow did not. She discovered that Daylesford did not like to be seen with her. When abroad they had been inseparable; now, though the intimation had never been clothed in words, she had slowly learnt, by trifling but convincing indications, that she must never expect to go out with him when he was in his own country. He never let any of his friends see her. He had been so little in England, that he had very few friends, or even acquaintances—not a dozen in all; but when any of them came to his house, Hester remained in her own rooms. This she preferred, and would have done without any hint from him; but it was painful to her. She sometimes saw him studying the advertisement pages of the 'Times;' she knew that from time to time he went to look at some house that he thought would do for her. She felt that she ought to take an interest in this search, and for his sake be willing to go, but she could not; for it seemed to her that it would be taking the first step towards saying farewell to him for ever. Her situation was much worse when he became acquainted with the Trehernes. He had told her all about his first meeting with Miss Josephine. Hester had been very uneasy that night about Daylesford himself, and had sat for hours almost despairing of his return. When he did return from his expedition to Lorne Gardens with Zeph, he had told the tired and anxious woman, whom he found waiting for him, what an adventure he had met with during the fog, and what a beautiful girl he had seen. He had told her of his subsequent meetings with the family, and of their visit to the castle, and then he had seemed to avoid speaking of them. He had seemed to avoid meeting them too, and had stayed with her much more than he had ever done since they had been in England. They had even begun to paint once more, and she had been happier than she had ever expected to be again. That was in March —in March, when Zeph was so unhappy. In April, however, there was a change. He would do no more painting; when he was in the house he was silent and preoccupied, and when he went out, which he did continually, Hester greatly feared that he was with the Trehernes. She was almost certain that there had been a period during which he had struggled against the fascination which the beautiful Miss Treherne exercised over him. She was sometimes still more certain that this struggle was abandoned—that he had yielded, and meant to yield. What was a poor loving woman, who desired his happiness more than anything else on earth, to do? The answer readily presented itself to her, but she shivered at the mere thought. The beautiful Miss Treherne! To a plain woman beauty seems such an overwhelming power. Hester knew that she herself was not beautiful, and had never mourned the deficiency more than now. And yet she scarcely did herself justice, for though her face was one which at first sight might have been called plain, there was something in her expression which compelled every one to look twice. It was the beauty of goodness shining out of her bright, honest, and entirely sympathetic eyes. Her face was of the good old Cumbrian type, but with the strange contradiction of a perfectly smooth skin and fine complexion, in conjunction with strongly marked features; her lips had a curve or two more than usual among the daleswomen, and her forehead and eyebrows more shapeliness. Her face might be plain, but it was for ever redeemed by her eyes and the revelation they afforded of her nature. Her figure, too, was splendid in its youthful grace and vigour.

One sunny morning in April she was sitting in her own room, shivering with cold and dread of the starvation of heart and soul which would be hers if she had to bid farewell to the man whom as long as she lived she must love. 'I had not the slightest idea such a terrible thing as this could happen,' she said to herself. 'When once we loved each other, I thought it was for ever.' Her thoughts then turned to her quiet home among the Cumbrian hills, far away from this noisy, changeful London. 'If we had but stayed there, he would never have cared for any one but me. He says that he cares for no one but me now, but does he think I cannot see how he is changed?' She heaped more coal on the fire, for, warm as the weather was beginning to be, she could not feel warm. 'It is my heart that is so cold,' she thought. 'How shall I bear it if I have to live all the rest of my life feeling like this?' Once or twice she caught sight of some object in the room, but she turned away her eyes from it in pain. There was hardly anything in that room which she could now look at without feeling as if it stabbed her. No room could have been prettier, but almost everything in it had been bought expressly for her, and with special reference to her tastes and wishes. The walls were light and covered with water-colours of the lakes and mountains and waterfalls which she had known and loved from her youth up. There were two pretty white bookcases filled with books which he had given her; she had read and enjoyed them all. 'I ought never to have come here,' she thought. 'Never! I ought not to have left my home with Godfrey as I did; but, come what may, he has been good and honourable to me, and if he has not been able to go on loving me, it is only because he has seen some one more like what he really most admires. After all, what was I but a poor little village girl? My only merit was my love for him, and it is not worth much if it does not last to the end.' And she sighed a long sigh of pain, for she knew that, by lasting to the end, she meant being equal to the sacrifice of resigning him if his happiness demanded it. Then her memory began to busy itself with the past, a past not quite four years old, when she had first seen Daylesford. She was an orphan, having lost both her parents while still a child. They had left her nearly destitute, but she had been adopted by an aunt, the widow of a country doctor, who had died young. Mrs. Langdale (Hester's aunt) had stayed in the lake-side village where her husband had died, and gained her livelihood by letting lodgings; and Hester, who had been at good schools, and was well educated, and in every way above her station, did not make the smallest difficulty about playing the part of upper servant to the aunt who was doing her utmost to be kind to her. This was how Hester Langdale had made Daylesford's acquaintance. He and two or three other young men had gone to the lakes with a tutor, and pitched their tent at Mrs. Langdale's house on the shore of Derwentwater.

Daylesford was reading for his degree. The young men did a great deal of boating, mountain climbing, and walking, and spent the summer most pleasantly. Daylesford sometimes invited Hester to go on the lake in his boat, or to join him in some sketching expedition. She had much feeling for art, and was a charming companion, full of enthusiasm and love of nature, and simple and innocent as a child. After spending weeks in each other's company an attachment sprang up between them, though they scarcely admitted the fact even to themselves.

These peaceful lake-side villages are often full of subtle dangers, and fevers linger in them for months and even for years. And yet tourists come and go without one word of warning from the inhabitants, for the very word fever would scatter all the money-bringing strangers. Daylesford sat down to sketch a cottage with a lovely porch covered with roses, and not till Hester saw the completed sketch did he learn that three children were in bed

with scarlet fever inside that house—a fact
good Mrs. Langdale would assuredly have concealed.   He caught the fever, and the reading
party dispersed in hot haste, leaving Mrs.
Langdale and Hester to nurse the sick man.
In due time he recovered, and then came the
wrench of parting.

No sooner had he returned to Oxford and
gone in for his degree than he heard that both
Hester and her aunt had caught the fever from
him, and the next news was that the old lady
was dead, and Hester dangerously ill.   He
went back at once, and saw that she had the
best advice and care.   His return saved her
life ; she had been breaking her heart about
him, and did not care to get well, but she recovered from the very hour when she learnt
that he was in the village again.   At length
the time came when he must once more part
from her, but the thought of this renewed
separation was more than she could endure.
She was ill and weak, and she showed her
whole heart to him and entreated him never to

leave her. Daylesford at that time was only one-and-twenty, and could not marry. His father, who had always attributed all the misfortunes of his life to an early and imprudent marriage, had, when he made over a large sum of money to Mr. Blackmore for the use of his own wife and sons, inserted a clause in the deed which forbade either of the young men to marry before the age of twenty-five. If they did so they were to forfeit all share of any money left by him. The earl had died some months before, but his death had made no difference to Daylesford's prospects, for the papers on which everything depended could not be found, and though there was going to be a trial, that would probably end in disappointment. If he married Hester he would be penniless. He had told her so, but again she had wept and entreated him never to leave her.

He never went back to Oxford, but they went to quiet places in France, Italy, and Germany, and there they had stayed until about four months ago, when they had, as Hester thought, so unhappily decided to return to England.

At first Daylesford had been almost as much out of society as Hester herself; now she wondered where he spent his time—now she began to feel her loneliness.

On this particular day it seemed harder to bear than usual. Godfrey was out, she did not know where, and he had gone without a word or message. He did not come home to luncheon; she ate some in a duty-manner, and then went out into the park. The day was fine, and the heavy pall, which had hung above the great city nearly all the winter, had entirely withdrawn itself, and seemed un-likely to return for the next six months. Hester breathed freely, and began, though with a heavy heart, to take something of a landscape painter's interest in the beauty of the trees and grassy undulations. She longed to make a sketch. It was so wonderful to see a fine park lying like a green gem in a setting of miles upon miles of brick and mortar. And how crowded it was with people who, though not a stone's throw from the great highway and still within hearing of street cries and the heavy roll of omnibuses, could fancy themselves fifty miles from London! She walked until she came to a more reasonable frame of mind. It was folly (so she told herself) to try to measure Daylesford's feelings by her own. He was a man, and he had a thousand cares and interests, of which a poor little country girl could have no ken; it would be madness to expect him to be the same in London as he was abroad, and, if she wished to keep his love, she must be largely trustful and generous in her interpretations of his conduct, and not chafe him by watching his moods and spying out shortcomings in his affection. The open air, the bright sun, and direct intercourse with such nature as was to be found 'within the radius,' soon restored her spirits to a certain amount of buoyancy; she was depressed, but by no means despairing. 'I hope he loves me still,' she said; 'I shall believe he does until it is certain that he does not, and then—and then I shall go, and I hope I shall be true to my love, and never say one word to make him unhappy. But I cannot—cannot think such a martyrdom lies before me!' She sat down on one of the seats, for she was beginning to be tired. A nurse was sitting there already with two little girls—pretty, interesting little quick-eyed, quick-witted creatures—it was a pleasure to Hester to watch them. She might, perhaps, have enjoyed this harmless amusement for twenty minutes, when a fair, placid-looking lady came up and, bending over the nurse, said, in a whisper loud enough to be overheard, 'Henderson, I often tell you how much I dislike your sitting on these seats when you are out! I do wish you would remember what I say! How do you know what bad character you may be sitting by? Come!'

Hester's face flushed scarlet. Those chance words struck home with deadly precision, and made her realise her position more than anything that had ever yet occurred. They had been uttered merely in indignation at the nurse's disregard of a general order, and had no reference to Hester, whose appearance was all that was modest and womanly. The lady departed with her nurse and children. Hester sat still, trying to recover the blow. ' I know I have done wrong,' thought she ; ' but I do not feel wicked—perhaps I ought—perhaps God will never forgive me until I do; but it is hard to feel wicked when I know that I am, and always will be, as true a wife to Godfrey as if I were really married to him.'

She raised her eyes, and, though still at some distance, saw Daylesford and two young girls coming towards her. He was talking gaily, and walking with a brisk, light step, which betokened a light heart. He was walking between them, talking most to the one on his right hand, who was beautiful and refined as one of Raphael's Madonnas, while her sister was a Rubens-like beauty, with pronounced features and vivid colouring. The first must

surely be the girl whom Hester most dreaded;
how strange that she should appear just at this
moment! Hester's heart died within her.
There was the woman who might possibly
win him away from her! And not make
him happy!—was her next agonised thought.
Women can arrive at a very fair estimation of
each other's characters almost at a glance, and
Hester saw the truth. 'She does not love him,
but she will accept his love if he offer it, and
will go through life thinking little of the gift.
How cruel, how wickedly cruel and unjust it
is that that girl, who would marry any man
possessed of certain worldly advantages, should
come and take from me the only man in the
world I can ever love! I wish Godfrey had
been a poor man, and I had been able to work
for him, and keep him all to myself! Does he
really love her?'

But there was no time to answer that, or,
at all events, poor Hester persuaded herself
that there was not, for she was not prepared
to face the situation if compelled to admit that

he did. They were now very near; she wished to leave the spot before he came up, but dared not attempt to move lest her knees should bow beneath her, as they do in dreams when flight is the only means of safety. She was obliged to remain where she was, but she earnestly hoped that he would not see her. They came nearer and nearer, and at last were quite close. She had wished him to pass without seeing her, but now it seemed so horribly heartless and unloving of him to be able to come within a couple of yards of the place where she was sitting, without being aware of her presence, that she thought, if he did so, it must break her heart. They were laughing and talking gaily, and he was apparently so well pleased even with the Rubens-like girl, that Hester felt full of despair, for she could see that something was making him so happy that he was able to see good in everything. He never saw Hester, but the girl, who she instinctively knew was called Josephine, looked at her with an interest which

visibly deepened as she gazed.   Either she
was struck by something in Hester's eyes, or
she had received some mysterious intimation
from her own soul, that there on that wayside
seat was one whose fate was linked with hers.
Even that gaze with its torture came to an end,
and they went on their way and soon disappeared from her sight, but they left her full
of misery.   And yet she was far from believing
him false to her.   All that she feared was that
this beautiful Josephine occupied a dangerously
large place in his thoughts.   'Should I feel
this if I were married to him?' she thought;
' if I were, and we went to dinners and balls
together, I should have to make up my mind
to see him looking very happy with other
people; but if we were married I should have
a claim on his love.   If he took it from me for
a while and gave it to some one else, I should
be very miserable of course, but his house
would be my home, and I could stay in it and
love him all the same, and, somehow or other,
I think I should win him back again; whereas

now, if he loves her, all that I can do for him is to go away and never let him hear my name again.' Her own thoughts tormented her so that she could not sit still ; she hurried away as quickly as possible to the more unfrequented parts of the park, where, shunning every one, she walked about for hours, thinking of the dreary days which might be in store for her. If she lost him she would be entirely alone in the world, for she had not a single relative. Besides, had it been otherwise, she never could go back to them now. No ; she, a girl of two-and-twenty, would find herself penniless and friendless. She never knew how many miles she walked that day, but at last, when the light was waning, she, footsore and sick at heart, began to return to the house which, up to this time, she had called her home. That morning's thoughts had destroyed her sense of security on that point for ever. She was beginning to know that it was but a house in which she dwelt at the will of another. She was there because Daylesford loved her ; when his love came to an end, there was nothing left for her but to go. So she walked slowly back to his house, envying the happiness of almost every woman she met on her way. Some were with their children, some walking arm-in-arm with their husbands, and uttering the dullest platitudes about the state of the weather or of the roads; but the men they walked with did not seem to mind how foolish their remarks were, and were not ashamed to be seen in their company. Godfrey was ashamed to be seen with her. What did that mean? It could mean nothing but that to be seen with her would be a disgrace to him. She could have sat down on the steps of one of the great houses she was passing as she thought of this, and cried her eyes out. 'Is there no way of altering it?' she asked in her despair; but, alas! she knew that there was none. If even he married her, he could not now raise her, it would simply mean that he must sink with her. His future would be ruined. She had gathered so much as that from some words of his own about a certain friend of his. Almost every woman would even then refuse to know her ; and Daylesford was not the man to humble himself to know men whose wives declined to know his. If he married her, he and she would, for the most part, have to be content with each other's companionship ; and supposing, as she earnestly hoped would be the case, that he were one day to set about making some good use of his abilities, this social difficulty would hinder him at every turn. 'I knew I had done wrong to come to him ; but I thought we should love each other as long as we lived, and that that would make all right.' This was her ever-recurring thought; but the merest hint of Daylesford's changing his mind shattered this theory which she had built up. 'God help me ! What a thing I have done !' she exclaimed. 'I see no help on any side ! '

Her feelings were so overwrought and excited that, when the servant opened the hall door as politely and respectfully as usual, and it closed on her without some one coming forward to say, 'Go forth, this is your home no longer!' she found it difficult to restrain herself, and felt as if she must throw herself down and burst into a flood of happy, grateful tears. She passed by the doors of the downstairs rooms quickly; Daylesford might be in one of them, and she was not prepared to see him yet. Unless, when she did see him, he should say something decisive to her, he must not be grieved by the knowledge of how she had spent her day.

Half an hour afterwards, with all her tears washed away, and no trace of past emotion but an unusually calm restrained manner, she went into the room where he was. He was sitting with his back to her, not reading, not doing anything, but looking into the fire.

'You are thinking about something, Godfrey?' said she humbly, and hesitating to go nearer; she was beginning at every turn to fear that she might possibly be an intruder.

'Yes, I am thinking,' he replied; 'I am wondering what you can have been doing all day.'

This reference to the bitterness of the bitterest day of her life filled her eyes once more with tears. Tears were out of the question now—not for worlds would she have let one fall in his presence. She was still behind him, and with a sudden movement of her hand she dashed them from her eyes, and by a great effort kept back those that wanted to follow. She could do that, but she could not speak in her usual voice; her words came slowly and sounded rather solemn. 'You want to know what I have been doing all day,' said she, kneeling down by his side and taking his hand; 'I am not sure I can tell you that, for I have done so little.'

'Have you been thinking, too?' he asked kindly.

'Yes.'

'Of what?'

'Of something that I should like to say to you if I dared.'

'Hester,' he said, startled by the gravity of her tone, 'what is it? Surely you dare say anything to me, dear?' and with his free hand he gently tried to raise her head, which was bent down, but she would not show her face.

'Wait till I have said it,' she gasped; 'it is only a word or so.'

He laid his hand on her shoulder, and at first his touch gave her courage, for it was loving and protecting as ever, but the next moment its very kindness seemed to unnerve her. If she did not speak quickly she could not speak at all.

'My poor dear Hester,' said he, 'you have been worrying yourself about something. Has anything happened?'

'No, dear, nothing, only I seemed to fancy you loved me less. That might happen, you know,' said she sadly, 'and I must bear it if it did. Godfrey, be good to me, and if ever it does, don't shrink from telling me.'

'It has not happened yet, Hester,' said he, drawing her towards him.

'Thank God! Then promise to tell me when it does.'

'You are too much alone,' said he. 'How can such a thing as that happen?'

'Promise to tell me if it does,' she persisted.

'All right!' said he so cheerily that she seemed to feel all her anxieties flying away from her in a moment. She kissed the hand she had been holding in hers, and a warm glow of happiness began to steal over her. Then he made her still happier by saying, 'Don't let us talk of such foolish things any longer. I want to give you an account of what I have been doing all day. I went to Bond Street to see how your pictures look, and then I went to the club and wrote to Marmaduke and had luncheon, and after that I walked home by the park and met two of the Trehernes; I joined them and walked all the way home with them, and by that time I thought it was high time to come home to you.'

He had told her of his walk with Miss Treherne; he had been perfectly frank and open about it, and he spoke of her just as he would have spoken of any other acquaintance.

What a jealous, morbid, discontented fool she had been! 'Godfrey,' said she very humbly, 'you are far better than I am! I am afraid I have been unkind. Tell me something about Miss Treherne; tell me a great deal about her. I saw her to-day. I saw both of them. I was sitting on one of the seats in the park when you passed by.'

He understood in a moment some part of what poor Hester had suffered, and on the spot sacrificed to her his intention to drop into the 'Levity' about ten to have a few words with pretty Miss Zeph; he had promised to go, but not for worlds would he pain Hester further.

'I don't want to talk about her now,' he replied; 'another time I will. I want you to hear about your water-colours; that's what I have been wanting to tell you all the time. I have good news for you: two of them are sold.'

'Sold!' exclaimed Hester incredulously.

'Yes, sold. I went into Winthrop's this morning, and he has sold them.'

Hester's face was radiant. The sale of her

drawings seemed to set a seal on her success; her patient labour was rewarded.

'Winthrop wants more. You are to send him some more.'

'My dear Godfrey, I am so happy!' said she; 'now I shall work twice as well as before. Will he really send me twenty guineas?'

'I dare say he will pare it down a little before he parts with it, but he will send you something that looks rather like that sum; but what do you want with twenty guineas?'

'Oh, don't laugh at me! His paying me anything at all is so delightful! It makes me feel myself quite an artist.'

After dinner they spent a thoroughly happy evening in looking over folios of sketches and choosing drawings which Hester should finish for Mr. Winthrop. Daylesford himself sketched fairly well, but Hester's love of nature was much more intense than his, and she had looked at her north-country mountains until she knew them by heart. They criticised bits of composition; most of the scenes depicted had associations for both which they dwelt on with loving pleasure; they had not been so happy for months. Daylesford scarcely remembered that he ought at that very time to be at the 'Levity'—that he had promised to be there.

Once, and once only, was the serenity of the evening imperilled. Cheered by the success of her drawings, and happy in Daylesford's affection, Hester was emboldened to say something which she would otherwise not have ventured on. 'Godfrey,' said she, 'I wish you would let me do something; it is a thing I have often thought of, but until these drawings sold I never considered my work good enough. Let me do two drawings of Berkhampstead— I might do one of the castle, and the other of the church, or both might be views of the castle—I have never seen either, of course, but I know from all the photographs you have what good subjects they would be; I want to do them as well as I possibly can by taking pains, and then I will give them to you, and you shall send them to your brother. He need never know who did them, of course, but I am sure he will like to have them.'

Then, seeing that Daylesford was silent, and, as it seemed, perplexed by what she was saying, she began to hesitate too. 'Am I saying anything foolish? Could you not take me there? I thought you could do just as you liked there, and might perhaps take me with you for a day or two next time you went.'

'We will think about it,' said he nervously; 'I should like it, I am sure. The Trehernes are going, you know, when next I go——'

'Oh, Godfrey, I don't mean when they are there! Of course not then!' exclaimed Hester, with burning cheeks and heart transfixed by a fresh stab from her true love's own hand; but she was anxious to preserve the happiness of this happy evening entirely unbroken, and said, 'Let me go with you some time when you are certain to be quite alone.'

'Impossible!' said he. 'Hester dear,

don't ask such a thing.   I could not do it—it
is not my house.'

'You are taking the Trehernes.'

'Yes, I am, but——' and he could say no
more.

Once again that day she was brought face
to face with her true and utterly sad, base, and
most pitiable condition.   What he meant was
that no honourable man could insult an absent
brother by installing his own mistress in their
ancestral home.   For one moment after she
had realised in what a dilemma her request
had placed Daylesford, she felt as if she should
faint or die; her heart utterly failed her.   By
a mighty effort she mastered herself, and said,
'Godfrey dear, I begin to understand; I see
that you could not do it!   Don't distress yourself about it; I don't really wish to go there to
stay, but I do feel as if it would be a pleasure
to me to do some pretty drawings of the place
for your brother, whom, for your sake, I cannot
help loving; and I will do them; I will go
there some time without any one knowing who

I am, and I am quite sure you will humour me, and send them to him as a present from yourself.' And thus, by an effort which was little short of heroic, did the unhappy girl pretend not to remark that even the man who loved her best was compelled, when honour called on him to exclude from his brother's house all persons whose presence would disgrace it, to include her among the number.

CHAPTER XIV.

ROPES OF SAND.

Poor girl! put on thy stifling widow's weed,
And 'scape at once from Hope's accursèd bands;
To-day thou wilt not see him, nor to-morrow,
And the next day will be a day of sorrow.—KEATS.

DAYLESFORD'S heart was deeply touched by
Hester's sufferings, and for ten days or more
he sought no opportunity of seeing Zeph.
This was by no means the first time that he
had made a strong resistance to the fascination
she was beginning to exercise over him. For
weeks after his return from Berkhampstead he
had, as the reader knows, neither gone to
Lorne Gardens nor paid her any attention.
He had, as he told himself, cast his lot with
poor little Hester; he felt that he had acted
very wrongly, to use no harsher word, but

he would abide by his own act and be true to her. So he struggled manfully against the strong attraction he felt to Josephine Treherne.

Had Hester's little success inflamed his zeal for art, or was it simply good-fellowship that made him take out his colour-box once more and set to work? She sat at one table with a spirited sketch of the Castle of Bracciano before her, he sat at another doing his best to reproduce the blackness of the pine forests at Ravenna.

'Do you think Winthrop would ever care to buy one of my sketches?' said he, holding the one he was busy with as far as he could from him, so as to judge of certain points of composition.

Hester hastened to express her conviction that Winthrop would be very blind to his own interest if he did not.

'I am afraid there is no chance of it,' said Daylesford despondingly. No one enjoys the luxury of turning an honest penny so heartily

as those who are rich. 'I should like to do
something really good. Do what I will, every
one of my drawings looks pretty much alike ;
now each of yours has a distinctly independent
existence.'

'Yours are very good indeed !' replied
Hester, 'but they would be better still if you
were like me, and there were only two subjects
on which you ever cared to think.'

'What are your two ? '

'You ought to know,' she answered ; 'you
are one, and my painting is the other ; I don't
believe I ever think of anything else.'

'Working as you do,' said he after a pause,
'you will soon master all the difficulties of
painting, and then it will be nothing but an
amusement to you.'

Hester looked at him in much surprise, she
had not expected him to say that. That speech
showed the difference between them. He was
not one to eat his heart in the struggle to conquer
something which resisted all attempts at con-
quest. She would have worked like a galley-

slave to reach any goal she set herself. He would have worked fairly well, but each day would invariably bring an hour when he would push away his drawing-board and say that he had done as much as he felt inclined to do, and must have a change. That hour had come now, and the day was yet young. He had not pleased himself with a sky he had been trying to put in, but he had resisted discouragement for some time; now he said, 'I am going out, I am tired of this.'

'I mean to stick to my work,' said Hester. 'Come and tell me what you think of it.'

'It looks lovely! I'd give a great deal if I could get those effects as easily as you do.' He always implied that Hester obtained her successes by mere natural talent, and never took into account how hard she worked. 'I am going out,' he again said, but still he did not go.

'Where are you going?' she asked.

'Oh, nowhere in particular,' he replied. 'Indeed, I am not sure I shall go out, after all.'   He seemed always to be halting between two opinions.

One morning he came into Hester's room with a large blotting-book covered with crimson velvet with the Daylesford arms embroidered in gold on each side. It had a lock, and its key was a marvel of intricacy, having little indentations and big indentations, and various subtleties of invention for the better discomfiture of nefarious persons, though a lock was no longer necessary, as the seams of its cover had been cut open, and it now gaped in a somewhat unsightly manner. 'There!' said he; 'there, my darling, I present you with a collection of photographs of Berkhampstead Castle. They shall be your own, to have and to hold for——' but here he stopped suddenly, for he became aware that he was accidentally straying into what must be unacceptable hearing to her—the language of the marriage service. This having to be so careful not to hurt Hester's feelings was, however, a new feature, and took away much of the comfort of home life. 'Take them,' said he, as she seemed to hesitate, 'take them. I have duplicates, I dare say, and if not, I can easily get some; and there are two or three sketches and things—you may have them too.'

'Thanks, they are very pretty;' and then, to put him at his ease about her wish to see the castle, she said, 'I'll try to work up two good views of Berkhampstead from these sketches and photographs; how very kind of you to give them to me! But what has happened to this pretty blotting-book?' she exclaimed, for when she had it in her hand she saw what a condition it was in.

'Its seams have been cut open, that's all,' he replied; 'everything was more or less maltreated a year or two ago, when we were hunting for papers.'

'This can easily be put right,' said Hester; 'it's only the sewing that has been undone, I see—I'll sew it again for you at once.'

'Not for me,' he said, for he saw that she admired the embroidery, and he felt that she would be pleased if he gave the book to her—perhaps because the family escutcheon was on it, and having it, made her seem part of that family—perhaps for some other reason. 'Do it for yourself. I present it to you, with all that it contains.'

'Thank you, it is lovely! I never saw anything so well embroidered; but what a shame to cut it to pieces in this way!'

'It was my father's; if you hold one of the pages of blotting-paper to the light, you will see that he used it when he was writing his last letter to his lawyer. Look, there is one passage you can read quite easily; it seems like fate that that should be preserved in its entirety, while the rest is only fragmentary: "My poor wife, whom, strange as it may seem after all that has passed, I sometimes think of with a certain tenderness." There are two or three other bits which can be read, but there is nothing so connected as this. If the genuineness of the letter had been disputed, that page of blotting-paper would have established it. I thought I was " getting very warm," as children say, when I discovered it.'

' I don't wonder you did; but you ought not to give this book away!'

' Oh, yes, I ought. Take it—I hate the very sight of it—it reminds me of such a bitter disappointment! We all thought that there was a great chance of something being concealed beneath the velvet, so we cut it open, and soon saw a bit of white paper appear. I can recollect now how my heart began to thump against my side when I caught the first glimpse of it.'

' Poor dear Godfrey! and what was hidden inside it ? '

' Nothing was hidden. There was nothing at all but a lot of white paper. I suppose it was put there to wedge out the velvet cover, and make the embroidery stand up well and look handsome.'

' Of course you thoroughly examined the papers ? '

' Thoroughly examined them ! I should

think so; we held them to the fire, we put acids on them to bring out secret writing; you may see the stains and burns yet, for all the paper is still inside the folio. Yes, that's it. We did everything we could think of.'

'But was there no writing? Was there nothing?'

'Nothing but that pen-and-ink scribble of a plan of the castle which you have in your hand.'

'How miserably disappointing! But don't lose heart, dear, I am quite sure that you will find what you are in search of. I have a presentiment you will. It is only a question of time.'

He could not but remark that Hester was using the very same words that Miss Treherne had used on that last day at the castle. It was strange that they should both say the same thing.

'Miss Treherne said the same thing to me, almost in the selfsame words,' said he.

Hester recoiled. She had not supposed

that he would talk to Miss Treherne on such intimate matters as this—her eyes filled with tears. She bent over her drawing to hide them, she had not even a monopoly of the right to console him. 'Perhaps I ought not to begrudge him the comfort of having her sympathy,' thought she, but it was impossible not to feel pain. She felt shame too. 'I am always jealous and suspicious and envious now. I shall make Godfrey's life as miserable as my own.'

'What does Miss Treherne do all day?' she asked, for she wished to remove the impression that she could not hear her name without showing signs of emotion.

'Nothing that I know of. She has never been taught to do anything. She is like a pretty silver shell cast on shore by the waves on a bed of rough pebbles. She is quite different from the rest of her family. I am very sorry for her—very. I think I shall go and see her, I want to know when that book of her father's will be done.'

'You are going to Berkhampstead when it is,' said Hester, with faint apprehension in her tone. 'Is she going too?'

'Yes, and so is her mother.'

Hester did not speak.

'I shall not stay long myself,' said he reassuringly. 'You know I don't like being there. I shall go backwards and forwards;' and then he went out, and to the Trehernes.

Somehow or other after this, Hester and Daylesford had no more happy working days together. Next morning, when she got out her Bracciano, she as usual put out his Ravenna. His pine forests looked black enough to encourage any one who was straining after blackness as a merit, but he never so much as came into the room where his drawing was. He read his papers downstairs, and then went into the billiard-room and knocked the balls about a little alone, after which he left the house for the rest of the day, and he did the same for a fortnight or more. Sometimes he was out in the evening too. Hester was very lonely and sad, and had not the heart to go out. She worked hard at the drawings she was busy with, and tried not to be uneasy, but her heart was full of sadness and her spirit void of hope.

At last Daylesford said, 'Hester, to-morrow I am going to Berkhampstead.'

'For long?' said she; for though he had told her he should only be absent four days when last they had spoken of this visit, much, alas! might have occurred to make him change his mind since then.

'For four days at the most, perhaps only three.' She breathed freely, and said, 'I dare say it will do you good, dear.'

He thought he detected a faint accent of resignation, and after a hasty glance at her to see how she was looking, for he had not been paying much attention to her appearance lately, he said, 'Why don't you take a little run somewhere, Hester? Suppose you go to Brighton for a week, or to some pretty place on the Thames, and do a sketch for Winthrop?'

'If you are only going to be away for four days, I'd like to stay here. If I went away for a week, I should not be here when you came home.'

'I shall not stay longer,' said he decisively. 'In four days I shall be back. You look as if you were afraid of being dull—four days are nothing.'

Hester wondered how these four days would be got over—quickly enough if she were sure he loved her as much as ever ; but days of doubt and sadness have a way of seeming as long as months.

'I will write you two letters while I am away ; one the day after I get there, and the other you will receive the day I come home. Come, won't that do ? ' said he cheerily.

'That will do,' she answered gaily ; he was so kind that she would be a wretch not to respond. 'I shall miss you terribly, dear, but I shall not be dull.'

'No, you have your profession to follow now,' said he, with an encouraging smile. She smiled too and said, ' If you could give me a piece of real hard work to do for you, it would help to make the time pass more quickly than it will otherwise. I should like to perform a hard task for your sake, and to feel that every bit of progress I made was bringing me nearer to seeing you.' She was so sweet and so tenderly devoted to him that Daylesford could not help feeling that it was wrong to leave her.

' You should have lived in the days of witches and fairies,' said he, ' and then you would have had a room full of flax to spin in four days, or a lake as big as your own dear Derwentwater to empty out with a tea-spoon. What shall I give you to do? I can't think of anything.'

Hester could not think of anything either. They had been such a short time in the house, that everything was in good order. There were no cupboards or bookcases with the accumulation of years in the way of books to dust and put in order. All was trim and new and well arranged at Eleven Ambassadors'

Gate—there was no finding any occupation for the demon of unrest.

'I shall have to set you to spin ropes of sand after all. I shall copy Lord Soulis—you shall begin to-morrow, and you shall spin them till I come back.'

'I hope you are bound to me by stronger fetters than those—you won't stay more than four days, dear?'

'I am certain that I shall not.'

When he went away in the morning, she once more reminded him of his promise. 'This is Tuesday,' said she; 'you will be back——?'

'On Friday,' said he gaily, 'and you shall have a letter on Wednesday and one on Friday. Good-bye; you have plenty of time to write, so you may as well let me have a letter every day;' and so saying, he went.

She did not feel so unhappy as she had expected. Four days was a long time, but it would pass by, and she no longer feared Josephine Treherne. 'I will try to do the Berkhampstead drawings for his brother,' she thought, ' and then I shall feel more as if I were with Godfrey.' She began to study the sketches and photographs. It was but a poor way of setting about a work of art, but she did not know that. Her room was full of flowers grown in the Berkhampstead gardens and greenhouses—they helped her to realise the aspect of the place.

Wednesday came. She hurried downstairs expecting to find a letter on the breakfast-table, but she was disappointed. ' I must have made a mistake,' she thought, ' and he only meant to write one on Wednesday; I shall get my letter on Thursday.' But Thursday also brought her nothing. She wrote to him each day, and bemoaned her letterless condition. ' He will see how miserable I am at not hearing from him, and be sorry that he has forgotten to write—my Friday's letter will be a doubly long one!' But Friday brought her no letter at all. ' It is very naughty of him, dear fellow,' she thought, ' but I suppose, as he is coming home to-day, he does not see the use of writing.

Perhaps he is right, but I should have liked a letter.' She ordered a dinner she knew he would enjoy ; she took infinite pains to arrange the flowers for the table : she dressed herself in her prettiest dress, and wore an Indian necklace he had given her on her last birthday. 'He is coming to-day,' she said to herself; 'he shall see how happy his return makes me !' Then she went downstairs and sat waiting to hear the first sound of his carriage. But it was beginning to grow late. The train ought to have been in three quarters of an hour already, but trains are often late, and it was a long way to the station. Another half-hour passed, and she began to think he must have driven home, as he did the time before. The servant came to ask if she would not have her dinner.

'No, I will wait for your master,' she answered sadly.

'We all think my master is not coming, ma'am,' said the man.

'Why do you think so ? '

'He never does come without sending notice, and Mrs. Mason has had none. She had a letter from Mr. Carnegie this morning, but he said nothing about coming back—he would have been certain to name it if they had been coming.' Mr. Carnegie was Daylesford's valet.

'Why didn't Mrs. Mason say so to me?' asked Hester. 'She might have done so when I ordered dinner, and then I should not have expected your master, and have had this disappointment.'

'Please, ma'am, she didn't like—she didn't know but what you had had a letter fixing the time master would return. I said I had seen no letter from him, and Thomas said the same, but we none of us could be certain.'

Hester blushed painfully. How terrible it was that the very servants should know that she had not received a single letter from Daylesford since his departure! She could not speak, she felt so humiliated. What must they think of a woman whose husband treated her with such indifference? for she never supposed that even the stupid little scullery-maid was aware that she was no wife, and that one and all they despised her, and only kept up the fiction of her being Mrs. Daylesford because it suited their interests to do so.

'You had better have your dinner, ma'am,' said the man kindly; he could not help being sorry for her. 'Everything can be kept warm for master,' he added, seeing that she was not inclined to yield.

'I must not seem to make his coming home of such importance!' thought Hester, and down she went and pretended to eat. The soup she had chosen because it was a favourite with him seemed to choke her, and so it was with all she ate. 'Is there a post from Berkhampstead in the evening?' she ventured to ask at last; 'I have never had a letter at night, but there may be a post.'

'There is none from the castle itself, ma'am, but when it is important to get a letter here by the evening, the groom rides

over to the town—it's only a three miles ride
—and then we get it.'

'I shall hear in an hour,' thought Hester.
'Godfrey will know what I must be feeling at
not seeing him, and will either send a man to
the post or go himself; so much kindness as
that I am sure he will show me.'

But he did not, nor was there any letter
next morning. 'That means he is coming to-
day!' again said Hester, who was determined
to put the best interpretation on his silence.
The housekeeper came to hear what she would
have for dinner. Hester gazed at her as if
trying to read her inmost thoughts. She
watched every change of the woman's expression, anxiously weighed each word she
uttered, hoping to see some look or hear some
word which would show that Mrs. Mason had
heard from her friend the valet, and knew
whether her master was coming that day or
not. Hester longed to be able to say, 'Has
Carnegie written to you? Is your dear master
and mine coming home to-day?' Alas that,

for the sake of that wretched thing called dignity, she must deny herself the comfort of putting this question!

And yet it was answered, and abundantly answered, by Mrs. Mason's demeanour. He was not coming! Hester knew it only too well. Mrs. Mason had allowed her to order a perfectly plain dinner, just what was wanted to keep a poor little creature like herself alive, and nothing more. She would not have done that if her master had been coming home. She would have said, 'Excuse me, ma'am, but Mr. Daylesford likes this, or Mr. Daylesford never seems to enjoy that when I have prepared it for him.' Hester knew her ways so well that she was convinced he was not coming that day, and it was Saturday; so now there was no hope until Monday. Alas! on Monday his return was as uncertain as it had been on Saturday. Days passed by, the four became ten, and still he neither came nor wrote. She grew pale and thin, and was too unhappy to do anything. She could not write to Daylesford. How could she write when he no longer loved her? Once a day, and once only, she roused herself, and that was to see Mrs. Mason. That good woman's heart ached for the unhappy girl whose face had, as she said, become 'all eyes,' and who 'seemed to be hanging on every word she opened her lips to say.' Mrs. Mason knew what Hester was longing to hear, and though she usually had a strong opinion about 'such good-for-nothing creatures as that young woman upstairs, being fit for nothing better than being put upon the kitchen fire and burnt!' yet, somehow or other, when she was in the criminal's presence her heart was melted, and she found herself wondering 'how a gentleman, for to be a gentleman as Mr. Daylesford really was, could take and treat a poor girl he had once made so much of, so downright badly as he was treating her!'

CHAPTER XV.

WHAT HAVE I DONE?

The sweet land laughs from sea to sea,
Filled full of sun.—SWINBURNE.
Piling roses upon roses evermore.—BROWNING.

IN February, when everything was cold and unlovely, Daylesford and the Trehernes had travelled through frost-bound lanes to Berkhampstead; and now that beauty had broken loose again, and all green things were rejoicing in having freed themselves from encumbering sheaths and being able to revel in sunshine and soft air, the same party made the same journey, but they used the grim iron way. Even viewed from the train, however, there was enough to make a town-keeping girl inclined to do nothing but gaze out of the window. Zeph had never before seen the

country early in June. It reminded her of
the scenery of the 'Lyceum,' but was a thousand times more beautiful ; and when she left
the train and began to drive through country
lanes to the Castle, and for the first time smelt
the perfume of wild roses and honeysuckle,
her delight was still greater. She felt all
the pleasure of a child, and wanted to stop
every minute to capture some particular rose,
being quite sure that it was an exceptionally fine
one, and that never again would she have a
chance of making such a beauty her own.
Daylesford humoured her as much as he could,
but Mr. Treherne was in a hurry to reach his
journey's end.

'Zeph dear, don't admire any more roses
and want them,' whispered Mrs. Treherne,
while Daylesford was pricking his fingers in
the hedge.

'I'll wear these dear crumpled-up pink
ones to-night,' said she ; ' and now I'll have no
more, thank you.'

Immediately after luncheon Mr. Treherne

begged, as the greatest favour which could be shown him, to be taken to the muniment-room. What a contrast to the sweet fragrance of hedgeside roses was the odour of mouldering parchment which issued forth the moment the strong door was unlocked!

'How very disagreeable this damp smell is!' said Daylesford.

'Disagreeable!' echoed Mr. Treherne, snuffing it up with much enjoyment; 'it is delicious! It may be from association, but I find it delicious!'

He was at work again in less than half an hour, and yet if he had been asked about it, he would have said that he had been obliged to sacrifice a very large portion of the day to the necessity of being polite to his host. He was now going to work as a paid official—he was to have so much per annum until his task was completed, and probably no one employed on such terms but an antiquary would have insisted on cutting the period of employment, and consequently the amount of his pay, short

by working so early, so late, and so con-
tinuously.

Daylesford was once more Zeph's only companion. They strolled about the garden a
little before dinner, and a great deal afterwards;
for there was light enough then to visit beds of
flowers, and half see them and half guess at
what they were by their scent, and Zeph liked
to explore tracts of shadow, and to wonder at
the length of time certain streaks of sunset
colour lingered in the sky, and at the immense
size of the castle as night stole on.

'How strong and big and forbidding it
looks!' said she; 'how terrible it would be to
be out here and to know that everything one
wished for was inside that great mass of
masonry, and that never by any chance could
one get in! What black shadows it casts!'

They strolled about the garden till they
were tired, and then they went in and talked
until they were tired again. Zeph slept soundly,
and at seven awoke to wonder where she was.
The garden was bathed in light mist, through

which the sun was struggling to make its way.
She could see Phillis Arnold's grave, with every
branch of the cypresses tipped by fresh green
shoots; she could see the heavy-headed roses
bending under the weight of the dew; she
could open her casement window and gather as
much white jessamine as she wanted. 'The
country in June is simply a paradise!' thought
she, 'and the country as seen from a castle is
something better still!' She sat gazing out of
her open window until the gong sounded.
Daylesford had been downstairs a long time,
hoping to renew the conversation of the night
before. Zeph liked talking with him very
much, but she never sought his society. She
looked as sunny as the day itself when she
entered the breakfast-room dressed in white,
and wearing a sprig of jessamine gathered from
her own window.

'What a delicious day!' she exclaimed;
' I have never known such a day as this: have
you, Mr. Daylesford?'

It was very beautiful, but he had known

many such—he could easily understand that Zeph had not, for even the June sun cannot work wonders, and must have something beautiful to shine on if it is to make a good impression; in Lorne Gardens there was nothing.

'You will find the garden and park a thousand times more beautiful now than they were when you were here before,' said Daylesford to Mrs. Treherne.

'But I did not see them when I was here before, Mr. Daylesford,' said she, turning her mild, slightly bewildered eyes on his. 'At least, I only saw what was visible from the windows.'

'Didn't you? To be sure, when you were here before, it was much pleasanter to take your exercise in exploring the house.'

'But I did not see the house either,' she replied despondently. 'I almost think, if I could make a little time, I should like to see something of the principal rooms and picture galleries this time.'

Daylesford was shocked—it had never before occurred to him that this poor lady was really too much of a slave. She was meek, loving, and unselfish, and she reaped the usual reward of such virtues—no one showed her any consideration; no one ever imagined that it cost her any effort to practise them.

'I shall have great pleasure in showing you the house myself,' said he kindly, 'and the garden and grounds too; and as it is so fine, perhaps Mr. Treherne will dispense with your company awhile this morning?' Daylesford was distressed to think of her having been shut up in the library day after day with the mouldy air of the muniment-room forcing its way into her lungs for want of any better.

But Mr. Treherne did not look as if he liked that arrangement.

'You will spare Mrs. Treherne?' said Daylesford; 'you will be so busy, you won't miss her.'

'I shall be busy,' he replied severely. 'Work was what brought me here, and it must be done.'

'Yes, of course it must, Edward; I'll stay,' began Mrs. Treherne.

'Won't I do for once, father?' asked Zeph. 'I'd like to be of some use to you, and I never shall if you don't teach me.'

'I like your mother best; but if she wishes to go out——'

'I don't,' interrupted Mrs. Treherne. 'I'd much rather——'

'I knew it——' began her husband.

'Oh, but you must both of you humour me for once,' interposed Daylesford. 'I can't give up the pleasure of escorting Mrs. Treherne about; you really must let her come.'

'Very well,' said Mr. Treherne reluctantly 'I must make Josephine do, I suppose;' and taking his daughter's hand in his, he led her away.

'Now let us begin our rounds at once,' said Daylesford. 'Perhaps we had better do the house first.'

'My conscience tells me that I ought not to take this step,' said Mrs. Treherne, with as

much earnestness as if she were about to elope
with her host.   'I really ought not!'

'Oh yes, you ought, dear Mrs. Treherne;
I will not allow you to change your mind.
Miss Treherne will be able to do all that your
husband wants,' said Daylesford.

'That's just it, Mr. Daylesford; that is what
makes me anxious.   In reality he wants almost
nothing, and I am afraid she will soon discover
that, and not have patience to sit idle as I
do.'

'Don't think about them,' said Daylesford
'You will see that all will go right.'

All did go right—Zeph never knew how
—perhaps because her mind was so full of all
kinds of thoughts, that its activity was reduced
to the level of her mother's, and she was able
to find his pen, and tie up documents, or undo
knots, when he asked her, mechanically.

'You are a dear, good girl, Zeph,' said he,
after a while, with a bright smile of affection.
She was so delighted with this that she began
to understand what was the reward for which

her mother worked, and to feel that it would not be absolutely impossible for her to bind herself in the same fetters.

Luncheon-time came, but Mrs. Treherne was so tired with her unusual exertions that she had a headache; so, in spite of Daylesford's efforts to lure Zeph out of doors, she would go back to her father, and Mrs. Treherne went to rest awhile. This was a great deal more than Daylesford had bargained for. He was anything but pleased. If she went back to the library he foresaw that he should see nothing of her till dinner-time, and he followed her to the library door and told her so.

'I am sorry,' said she, ' but I must go.'

' At any rate, we will have another walk in the garden after dinner; promise me that.'

' Yes,' she answered, and disappeared. So he went to Berkhampstead on business which would otherwise have been postponed.

About five, however, Mrs. Treherne felt better, and returned to her post; so Zeph went to walk in the garden. She walked through the grounds towards the church, and met Mrs. Scatcherd coming to call on her.

'I heard you were here, dear,' said that lady, 'and thought I would lose no time in coming to see you. Don't offer to go in. I'll walk about here with you; the air does one good. I have had such a day with some of those wretched boys; but don't let us talk of them. It is the greatest folly to talk of things you want to forget, and yet people always make a point of doing it. How lovely you look! How do you think I look?'

Zeph returned her compliments, and asked after the doctor and the Vincents, and what Mrs. Scatcherd had been doing; and then that lady said, 'Why is Mr. Daylesford not with you?'

'Why should he be with me?' inquired Zeph.

'Young people generally do contrive to be together. I saw him going to Berkhampstead an hour or two ago. He is a nice fellow! He must be lonely, though; it is a charity of all of you to come here!'

'Oh, but we do not come in that way,' said Zeph hastily; 'my father is arranging the documents in the library—muniment-room, I mean—for him. He is engaged to do it, and I don't see why Mr. Daylesford need be so lonely—he has relations; there is a Mrs. Daylesford who stays with him in Ambassadors' Gate—why does not she come here with him?'

'My dear!' exclaimed Mrs. Scatcherd, with eager earnestness, 'you don't mean to say you know about that! That's a thing I should never have dreamed of naming to you if you had not spoken of it yourself. How could he bring her here? The whole neighbourhood would be up in arms; every one would cut him!'

'Has she done anything to offend them? Don't they like her?' asked Zeph, with perfect unconsciousness.

'Like her!' echoed Mrs. Scatcherd; 'but surely you cannot understand who she is?'

'That is just what I do not understand,' said Zeph; 'at first I thought she was his wife, and then I thought she was his brother's, but I am told that they are neither of them married. Is she an aunt of his? She might be an aunt, only I thought he told me his father never had a sister.'

Mrs. Scatcherd stared at her in amazement, and said, 'Then you did not know, after all. Well, the thing is half told now, so you may as well hear the rest of it: she is a girl who lives with him—they are not married.'

Zeph turned perfectly white—even her lips were white. 'You must be mistaken,' she stammered; 'you really must; she is called Mrs. Daylesford; I know she is!'

'That is nothing!' said Mrs. Scatcherd; 'what I have told you is the truth. Don't go and faint about it—you look so ill, you frighten me. I thought you knew, or I should never have said anything. Every one knows, every one here was very glad when he paid you so much attention at the ball, for they thought he was perhaps going to break loose from this horrible entanglement. I hope he will do so still; it will be the saving of him if he is really in love with you, and then he will get rid of this wretched creature. It seems she——'

'Hush, Mrs. Scatcherd! don't tell me anything about her,' said Zeph, making a great effort to speak. 'Don't tell me one word more, I ought not to have heard this. Excuse my saying it, but I must not let you tell me Mr. Daylesford's secrets; my father was very angry with me for listening to what you told me before.'

'I don't want to tell you any of Mr. Daylesford's secrets—I know none, indeed; this is no secret—every one knows it.'

'And people go on knowing him?' said Zeph, with cold scorn.

'Why not, dear fellow? Of course no one would be in the same room with her, horrible creature that she is—that is a very different matter! My dear, don't look so ill and so unhappy—he is not the only man who is living in this way ; the thing is common enough I am sorry to say.'

'Do not let us say another word about it,' said Zeph.   'How is Dr. Scatcherd ? '

' Oh, John is well—he is strong—it would be a very bad thing for him if he were not; but I must say one word more, just one word.   Do not be unhappy about this, dear; forget about it; the one thing to hope for is that our kind friend should marry some good girl whom he can love and respect.'

Zeph shuddered.

' If ever you marry him,' continued Mrs. Scatcherd, ' don't go and tell him of this conversation.   Promise me that.'

' I marry him ?   Never !   What do you take me for ? ' said Zeph through her angry tears.

' Oh, dear, dear ! what have I done?   I take you for a dear, good girl, who may be the means of saving him——Oh, here he is ! ' she exclaimed in much alarm, for she saw Daylesford shutting the churchyard door and beginning to follow them as quickly as he could.

'I cannot see him!' said Zeph hastily; 'I won't. I'll say good-bye and go in;' and without giving Mrs. Scatcherd a chance of detaining her, she hurried back to the house much too quickly for Daylesford to overtake her, and shut herself in her own room. Her mother was in the library, there was no one to whom she could speak. She did not shed one tear, she no longer felt inclined to shed any. She was stung to the quick. She felt disgraced by his notice, ashamed that he should like her. She had never once conceived it possible that she could know a man of this kind. She would henceforth avoid him. She would show him that he was mistaken in thinking that she was the kind of girl he liked. When the time came to dress, she put on her evening dress with stern calmness, and slowly descended the stairs with her mother, for whom she had waited.

'Why did you run away when you saw me,

Miss Treherne?' said Daylesford, with a most injured manner, as soon as she entered the drawing-room. 'I wanted to have the pleasure of walking back to the house with you.'

'I was tired. My head ached. I was in a hurry to get back,' said she nervously but very coldly.

He observed—no one could have failed to observe—the coldness of her tone; he searched diligently for subjects of offence, but found none but this: she was cross with him for some implied reproach with respect to her conduct to her mother, and angry at having been forced to take her place in the library that morning. It seemed very unamiable to begrudge her mother the few hours' pleasure this had procured her.

'I am afraid your morning's work has tired you,' said he.

'On the contrary, I enjoyed it,' replied Zeph severely; 'I hope father will always let me stay with him.' The tone of her voice again surprised him; he thought it advisable to plunge into general conversation; he would 'have it out' with her when they had their walk in the garden after dinner. But when that time came she declined to go. She was very sorry, but she had been out before dinner and was tired; and when Mr. and Mrs. Treherne retreated to the library at nine o'clock as usual, she rose to go to bed, and avoiding all opportunity of being alone with him, and, as he thought, showing some repugnance to shaking hands, she retired to rest. He sat puzzling himself about this change in her demeanour, and used up the time he had meant to have given to writing to Hester in vain efforts to understand it.

Next morning she was just the same, and when her father went into the library she followed him. 'Find me something to do, dear,' she pleaded; 'I liked being with you yesterday, and want to stay here to-day.'

He stroked her hair and said, 'There is work enough for all of us, my darling.' So she sat down by the table, prepared to make notes of anything he told her; this gave her more than enough time to think. Mrs. Treherne sat by them, happy in their company.

'I seem to have got hold of a letter that does not belong to me,' said Mr. Treherne after a while, doubtfully fingering one addressed to Mr. Daylesford.

'Don't disturb yourself about that, dear, you will soon have a chance of giving it to him, no doubt,' said Zeph, eyeing the letter and the pretty writing of Mr. Daylesford's correspondent with great disgust and dislike.

'I was not thinking of doing anything,' said he, with his usual accuracy. 'He is sure to come soon, let it lie till he does;' and so saying, he returned to his work.

The neighbourhood of this letter disturbed Zeph; she knew who had written it. She flung a sheet of paper over it, and tried to forget that it was there. After a while Daylesford came and asked Zeph if she would go to the conservatory with him, he wanted to show her a very fine orchid which was now in bloom.

'No, thank you,' said she; 'not this morning.'

'Then I think I will ride over to ——,' said he, naming a place about twenty miles off. Alas! who was there to offer any objection to this if Zeph did not? and she appeared to be absolutely indifferent. He turned to leave the room with an offended air. Zeph remembered the letter which Mr. Treherne had already forgotten; she pushed it towards her father.

'Oh, Mr. Daylesford, I have carried off one of your letters!' he exclaimed; 'I cannot imagine how, but do forgive me.' Zeph studiously avoided seeing how Daylesford looked when he saw the writing.

He did not return till late, and saw nothing of the Trehernes till next morning. No one seemed to have missed him. This was Friday, the day he had promised to go back to London. If things had been different he might possibly have stayed where he was till Saturday, but as it was he would go—he had been too unsettled to write to Hester, so he would go—at all events for a week or so.

'I am going back to town by the five o'clock train,' said he. Mr. Treherne was the only one of the party who showed any interest. 'You of course will stay here with Mrs. Treherne and your daughter as long as you can. I will give the servants orders to look after your comfort.'

Zeph insisted on accompanying her father and mother to the library when they went, and there she would probably sit in dulness and comparative idleness while the sun shone brightly and all outside that room was gay. Daylesford made no attempt to prevent her—he knew that it was impossible. While he was wondering how to employ himself, Dr. Scatcherd came to ask him to go to Oxford with him for an hour or two. Why not? he could go back to London from Oxford. So Carnegie was ordered to pack his master's portmanteau, and, after a few words of farewell to the Trehernes, he went.

The 'Times' did not arrive at the castle till noon; soon afterwards the butler brought it to the library to Mr. Treherne with a grave face. 'I want to show you this, sir,' said he. 'I am afraid my master will be in a terrible way!'

It was a telegram in large print : 'Appalling earthquake in the Icarian Islands! Alarming loss of life at Santa Eulalia! Grave apprehensions as to the safety of the Governor! Government house in ruins! Repeated shocks!'

Pale as Mr. Treherne always was, he turned paler. 'The Governor is Mr. Daylesford's brother,' said he in a dismayed voice; and then he and his wife and daughter huddled together over the paper to see if they could extract a ray of hope from it. Two large round tears rolled down Zeph's face. The meagre words of the telegram conveyed nearly as much as the complete account; the rest was mere amplification.

'Do you think that there is any hope of his being rescued alive from the ruins of his house?' she asked. No one dared to hope much, but there might be room for hope. A shock had fallen on the Trehernes. Zeph could do nothing but weep silently; even Mr. Treherne could not work well. The evening's post brought two letters from Daylesford, one to Mr. Treherne, one to Zeph. He read his aloud: 'A crushing blow has fallen on me. My dear brother may be dead. I am going at once to Santa Eulalia. I shall cross by to-night's boat.' It was written in pencil, and bore marks of extreme haste.

'Did you say that you had a letter from Mr. Daylesford too, Zeph?' asked Mr. Treherne.

'Yes, dear; I'll tell you what he says.' But when she opened it she seemed much confused, and at last said, 'I was wrong. No, I have not had a letter from him.'

Presently she stole away to her room. The letter was addressed to her by Daylesford in pencil, as was that to her father, but when she had opened it she read, 'I cannot come home to-day as I promised, for I must at once go to Santa Eulalia to my brother. The newspapers will tell you what has happened. Dear Hester, ever yours,

'G. D.'

CHAPTER XVI.

THE PENCILLED LETTER.

Best of my life, farewell, since we must part,
Heaven hath a hand in it.—Duchess of Malfy.

No, no, you have dismissed me, and I go
From your breast houseless; ay, it must be so.—Keats.

On July 15, five weeks after the day when he went to Berkhampstead with the Trehernes, Godfrey Daylesford once more entered his London house. He did so feeling much apprehension, for he had not received one line from Hester since he had left England, and yet he had sent her both letters and telegrams. 'How is your mistress?' were his first words.

Thomas looked blank. First he stared at his master and then at Carnegie, but he did not attempt to answer. Daylesford repeated the inquiry. 'Better speak to Mrs. Mason, sir,' said he; 'she knows best.'

'Mrs. Daylesford is not here, sir,' said that personage, when she appeared in answer to his summons; 'she left ten days after you did, sir. She seemed much cut up about receiving no letters, sir.'

'Letters!' exclaimed Daylesford sharply; 'she must have received letters; I wrote to her before I left England to tell her why I was going, and I wrote again soon afterwards. Besides, she had telegrams from me.'

'None of them came here, sir; at least not while she was here. A telegram came about ten minutes after she had left the house; you will find it upstairs on Mrs. Daylesford's sitting-room table, sir, and three letters from you which came after it. But she never saw any of them. We none of us knew you had left England, and we didn't know, for some time after you were gone, what an alarm you had had about the Governor's safety. That, sir,' said the housekeeper, who was glad to take this opportunity of airing a grievance of long standing, 'was because of all the newspapers going direct to the castle as soon as you went, instead of coming here.'

'Did Mrs. Daylesford not know that at one time I was afraid my brother was killed?'

'No, sir, she did not. She never went out of the house all that time, so she had not even the chance of getting to know from seeing the placards, and no one came here to tell her any news.'

'But what must she have thought?'

Mrs. Mason shook her head, and eagerly seized this opportunity of making him uncomfortable. 'She was terribly unhappy, sir. The sight of her when she used to watch my face to see if I knew anything about you, or when you were coming home, was quite enough to break one's heart. She was so quiet and gentle, and so full of trouble.'

'But how did she go, and where?'

'I can tell you how, sir, but I cannot tell

you where. She sent for me one morning, and said, "Mrs. Mason, I have decided to leave this house."

'"A change will do you good, ma'am," said I, though I felt sure she did not intend to come back.

'"Perhaps it will," said she, making up her mind to let me think she was only going away for a time. "Will you take one of the maids with you, ma'am?" I asked. "I can easily spare you one while every one is away." "You are very kind—most kind," said she humbly, "but I must go alone. May Thomas get me a cab?"

'"Will you not use the carriage, ma'am?" said I. She shook her head very sadly, and said, "No, not the carriage, let me have a cab." So I sent for a cab, and then I went upstairs again to see if I could be of any use to her, or show her any kindness. She was walking round and round her sitting-room, wringing her hands and looking at the books and pictures. I said a few words of sympathy of some sort, I hardly know what, she made me feel so sadly. But she spoke up very quickly and said, "Don't pity me, Mrs. Mason, I cannot bear it; please don't, or you will make me cry." There were two small parcels on the table addressed to you. "Mr. Daylesford will find them when he comes home," said she, in a trembling voice. "May I ask you where you are going, ma'am?" said I; "there may be letters to forward." "Oh no, he won't write now," said she; "but post this letter when I am gone, and it will give him my address." And she gave me a letter addressed to you at Berkhampstead. Perhaps you have had it, sir?'

'No, I have not; no letters have been forwarded. Do you suppose it is still there?' asked Daylesford hastily, and he rang the bell. 'Thomas,' said he, 'go at once to Berkhampstead. If the trains suit, go by rail; if not, ride; but you must be back here to-night. I want all the papers and letters which are lying there for me brought here at once.—And now, Mrs. Mason, have you anything more to tell me?'

'Nothing but things of the same kind, sir. She went on walking about and taking notice of all the things she had been used to see and to care for, until the cab arrived, and then she came to me. She held out her hand and said, " Good-bye, Mrs. Mason; you have been kind to me when no one else was, and I shall never forget it." But when she stooped down and kissed my poor old hard-working hand, you might just have knocked me down with a feather, sir, for all I am such a big woman. She hadn't been gone ten minutes before a telegram came which we made sure was from you, sir. Poor lady, it came too late. I was miserable all that day, and the next, and so I am still, whenever the thought of her comes into my mind.'

'Did she leave no letter for me?'

'No, sir, none here. She wrote to the

castle, where she made sure you were. That is all I have to tell you, sir, except that I wish to leave you this day month.'

Daylesford, who was thoroughly conscious of the reprehension she meant to convey, went upstairs, wondering whether she was taking her departure because Hester had been there or because she had left. Her sitting-room looked very desolate. Every article of furniture was in its exact place. Three unopened letters and one telegram from himself were arranged with symmetrical precision on the table; other correspondents she had none. There were two parcels addressed to him. One was a flat one, which he opened. It contained two sketches of Berkhampstead. The other was a small key-box. It opened by a secret spring with which he was familiar, but there was nothing in it but keys. She had left all the books he had given her, and the pictures on the walls were hers too. Daylesford was miserable. Instead of a happy home-coming, he had returned to a house filled by a haunting sense of the suffering and sorrow he must have brought on an unhappy girl who had none to show her any kindness if he stood aloof.

Even if Daylesford's grief and regret had not been too acute to allow him to settle down to any occupation until his messenger returned, he was not a man who had much power of finding employment for himself on the spur of the moment. He began to wish he had gone to Berkhampstead himself. 'But no,' he thought, 'I ought to stay on the spot, to be ready to go to her at once when I get her letters and learn where she is. I might have lost some time if I had gone there and had seen the Trehernes. By-the-bye, I suppose they are there. It is strange how little I know about every one. I think I will go and ask in Lorne Gardens. I have time to do that before dinner.' He hailed a hansom, and soon was there.

'Master and mistress and the eldest young lady are away in the country,' said the maid, 'staying in a nobleman's castle. The two young ladies are at home, and so is Miss Seaton.'

Daylesford remembered that Mrs. Treherne had told him that she had invited Miss Seaton, a cousin of hers, to take care of her daughters while she herself was away, and how astonished he had been that it should have occurred to the Treherne mind that such a step was at all necessary. He thought he would go in and ask news of the family—it would help to pass the time. The three ladies were at work. It was evident at the first glance that Miss Everilda Seaton had improved the girls' appearance. They were quietly dressed, and their manner was not so hoydenish as before. Miss Everilda (as she liked to be called) was a small, bright-looking, bird-like lady, of forty or thereabouts, with large blue eyes and a profusion of light brown hair. She had very pretty white hands and a very sweet voice. Her manners were even too refined and elegant, and her sentiments were often much above the range of her fellow-mortals.

'Yes, father and mother and Zeph are still at Berkhampstead,' said Polly, 'and being so long away has done them so much good; they do look so well. And do you know, Mr. Daylesford, Zeph is looking quite pretty!'

Daylesford smiled; he expected that when he saw Miss Treherne he should feel inclined to use much stronger language than this.

'And, Mr. Daylesford, what do you think? No, you can never guess. We have all been to Berkhampstead while you were away. We never enjoyed anything, so much in our lives. We went for a long day, and spent it with Zeph seeing the park and the castle. Miss Everilda went with us, and she thought everything beautiful too, and you know she has seen a great many more beautiful places than Agnes and I have.'

'It was most beautiful,' sighed Miss Everilda; 'most ideally beautiful. Such a park! Such a pleasaunce! Such lovely green glades! The place quite inspired me, and I felt as if I could have written a poem worth something.

But it's no use; I am such a poor tongue-bound creature!   I have all the fine ideas, but I cannot bring them out—I cannot bring them out!'

'I feel so sorry that this visit took place in my absence,' said Daylesford politely, 'but I do hope you will consent to repeat it.'   All three expressed much gratitude, and all three looked charmed with him and the kindness of his manner.

'We were so glad when we heard of the Governor's safety, Mr. Daylesford.   You must have been terribly anxious.   What a miracle his escape was!'

'How did it really happen?' asked Agnes.

'At the moment of the earthquake he started to his feet and got as far as a strongly built doorway, and the walls fell on both sides of him, leaving him standing upright and safely built in.   Of course the great danger came when he had to be dug out.   He really had a very narrow escape!'

'What a subject for a great dramatic picture!' exclaimed Miss Everilda. 'I see it all —his grand figure standing nobly unmoved amid the wreckage of his home—his heart feeling nothing on his own account, but dread of what you must be suffering.'

'He must have wanted to get out though,' said Daylesford, with a kind smile.

'Ah, yes, to be useful to his distressed subjects. I see it all—I feel it all. But it's no use my seeing or feeling things so vividly; when the time comes to write, my ideas vanish, and every faculty I have is benumbed.'

'Would you mind telling us something about the island which your brother governs?' asked Polly, with signal disregard of the would-be author's lamentations. But Polly was always practical.

'He governs five or six, but he lives on the principal one, which is called Santa Eulalia. When I first saw it early in the morning of a very bright day, it looked baked white in the heat. We were in the harbour, and were not allowed to land till the captain had gone on shore and proved that we had a clean bill of health, so I had time to inspect all that was left of the town from the harbour. Rather ugly tall houses were built irregularly about the shore, and there was literally not one left standing that had not one or two great zigzag rifts and cracks in its walls; of course many were nothing but heaps of stones. The inhabitants were all camping out on the hills in funny improvised tents, and every time a cock crowed or a bell rang, they believed another earthquake was coming.'

'Did you not note down your thoughts?' inquired Miss Everilda. 'You could have described it adequately. You are not like me —I have the thoughts, but I never can bring them out.'

'I had no particular thoughts beyond the fact that the earthquake must have been a most appalling thing, and that I was very impatient to see my brother. But he soon came, and we set quarantine regulations at defiance.'

Every one was silent for a moment. Then

Miss Everilda spoke. 'Ah, what sights you must have seen as you went through the town with him! Once happy homes turned into heaps of stone, great forest trees lying up-rooted!——'

'Oh, no,' interrupted Daylesford, 'there are no forest trees on those islands—there are never-ending hedges of aloes, but no trees to speak of.'

'That, too, conjures up great thoughts. But, Mr. Daylesford, did you see no sign of the dread enemy but the wrecked houses? Were there no vast chasms which revealed the interior of the earth smouldering in a red glow?'

'There were any amount of little bits of sulphur lying about, which were mightily suggestive of the bottomless pit, but I expect they are always there, and I saw hot springs bubbling up, but they are always there too.'

'Oh dear, oh dear! You are sure you wrote nothing? Even I, hearing it all only second-hand, feel inspired. Not that it is any use; more's the pity!' she added mournfully.

Daylesford beat a retreat, and yet he hated going back to Ambassadors' Gate so much that he could almost have stayed where he was. His messenger did not return until late. He brought a number of letters, among which were four from Hester. The last of them contained these words:

'I am leaving this house for ever, to-day. I have waited and hoped for some sign that this step was unnecessary, but your silence answers me, and tells me that the time has come when I must go. I am so unhappy as to have lost what was more to me than all else, your love. I sometimes wish you had spared me so many days of cruel suspense, and had told me at once what had befallen me. Dear Godfrey, let me call you so for this last time, I do not blame you. I know that this has not come to pass without you too having your share of suffering. Let me thank you for all your great kindness to me. Do not be unhappy about me; I shall work very hard and try to be content. I shall always think kindly of you. I have taken two or three of the books you gave me, and the colour-box, and all I need for my work. I thought you would like me to do this, and I like having these things. I have left the ornaments you gave me. I shall never want ornaments again, nor ever care to look well in the eyes of any one, now that you do not love me. Do not attempt to send me any of the things I have left. I am going where you cannot find me, and I would rather not have them. Good-bye. Thank you once more for all you have been to me.—Hester.'

Then there was one despairing clutch at hope in the shape of a postscript. 'Supposing that by any chance there has been some dreadful mistake, and you still love me, put an advertisement in the second column of the "Times" with these words: "Hester, you were wrong." I shall look in the "Times" every day for three weeks.'

This letter, alas! had not even been seen by him until the three weeks named by poor

Hester were gone by, and more than gone by. Her weary eyes had sought the longed-for announcement in vain. 'I can still do it,' said he, 'and I will.' Then he looked at the other letters. He opened one which had not gone through the post, and found in it an envelope addressed to Miss Treherne, The Castle, Berk-hampstead, in his own writing in pencil; only the 'Miss' had been torn off, leaving it doubt-ful to whom the letter had been directed. When Daylesford drew the letter out of this envelope, he saw that it was that which he had hastily written in pencil to Hester to tell her that he was going at once to Santa Eulalia. This explained everything. Hester had never received one line from him since he left Ambas-sadors' Gate to go to Berkhámpstead. He in his grief and confusion had addressed his letter to one of the Trehernes, and every letter he had written since he went abroad was lying unopened on the table upstairs. She had indeed been cruelly used! After a while, though with much indifference to their contents, he opened some of the other letters. There was a warm little note of congratulation from Mr. Treherne on his brother's safety and his own return, and as a postscript the words, 'I am so delighted that you had the happiness of finding your brother well.—Josephine Treherne.'

These words pleased him more than he could have believed possible. And yet he put the note which contained them on one side, and once more took up the pencilled letter which had never reached its destination. He little knew what an amount of embarrassment and trouble it had caused Zeph before it had at last found its way into his hands. Somehow, when he thought about it, he forgot to wonder how it had gone wrong, or who was the person whose name he had written on the envelope instead of Hester's; he thought only of Hester herself, and left all else on one side. If Zeph could but have known that this would be the case, what anxiety she would have been spared! She had felt that it would be wrong to destroy the letter, and yet she did not wish to be supposed to have seen it. She dared not tell her father or mother about it, and did not choose to take Mrs. Scatcherd into her confidence. She longed to solve the difficulty by flinging the wretched bit of paper into the all-purifying element, fire. Let it shrivel away out of sight, together with other dark and unlovely things. Ignorant as Zeph was, she knew that it would be wrong to do this, and the possession of these hastily written words, intended for the eye of another, disturbed her. Ought she to return the letter to Mrs. Daylesford? She could not bring herself to do so, even without a word of explanation. To the housekeeper at Ambassadors' Gate, then? That would not be the same thing. Besides, her own name, Miss Treherne, was written on the envelope, and the person to whom she forwarded it would know that she must have read it, for there was nothing to show for whom it was meant until the very end, where the name of Hester occurred. Zeph knew that she ought not to destroy the envelope in which it had been sent, for that

was wanted to show how the mistake had
arisen. She had no peace until she had decided
to tear off the 'Miss' and leave the name of
Treherne; that would tell him the letter's
history sufficiently, and he would surely not
dare to ask more. Having done this, she had
enclosed the letter in an envelope which she
addressed to Daylesford in writing as unlike her own as she could contrive to make it,
and laid it on the hall table, knowing that the
butler would carry it away, either to forward
to Santa Eulalia with other letters, or to keep
until his master's return, according to the in-
structions he might have received. That done,
though she had no idea that Hester's only
chance of ever receiving a letter from Daylesford again depended on how this scrap of paper
was treated, she felt as if a weight were
removed from her mind. And yet she could
never forget the chill that had come over her
when she had found what she was reading. Now,
after weeks of delay, it had come back with its
errand unsped, to the man who had on that

day of anguish been so glad to give a guard on the railway a sovereign for an inch or two of a well-used pencil and some writing-paper.

That very evening, July 15, Daylesford wrote to the 'Times' authorities, and requested that the four words which had been chosen by Hester should be printed in the second column of that paper for three weeks. Then he went to Winthrop's. Winthrop was the man who would probably be able to give him the information he wanted, for on Winthrop Hester no doubt depended for means of livelihood. Daylesford now asked Mr. Winthrop if he had any more of Miss Langdale's drawings.

'No, sir,' said he; 'I am almost surprised she has not sent me some. I was not long in disposing of those she sent me before, and I have had one or two gentlemen in my place who have taken a good deal of notice of them.'

'Have you had no communication with her since she brought them, then?'

'None but sending her a cheque.'

This was a thoroughly unproductive visit,

for Daylesford could learn nothing more. The advertisement, too, brought no response ; it appeared day after day, but all in vain. After five or six days had gone by, he began to feel assured that he had lost sight of her for ever, and he sometimes felt bitterly ashamed that this conviction did not make him more unhappy. And yet his house, which was filled with traces of her former presence, was most painful to him. She had taken away with her all her clothes, and every scrap of paper which could have revealed that such an occupant as herself had ever resided in the house. She had done this with such care that it must have been done designedly, and for his sake, and she had left things which when he gave them to her had made her cry with pleasure. These, however, were in all cases things on which no mark had been set which could prove that they had been hers. He did not like his house now that she was gone, and he could not raise his eyes from the ground without seeing something which brought an accusation against him. He spent most of his time at the club, and only went home to sleep, but when a week had gone by in this way he was tired. Sometimes, almost to his horror, he even found himself thinking that it was better that he should never discover her.

And yet it was strange that there was no reply from Hester. She had kept her word and gone where he had no chance of ever finding her. He began to give up all hope. Still he would continue to advertise. It was dreadful to think to what straits she might be reduced.

CHAPTER XVII.

A STRING OF PEARLS.

Peu d'œuvrage donne beaucoup d'amour-propre, beaucoup de travail donne infiniment de modestie.—BALZAC.

MISS EVERILDA SEATON had a large acquaintance among editors of magazines and weekly papers—at least she thought she had. Perhaps, as she generally introduced herself to these gentlemen by sending a copy of verses, and they kept up the acquaintance by writing to decline her contribution 'with thanks,' the friendship may not be considered warm; but as she always encouraged their advances by sending more verses, and as they always responded precisely as they had responded before, it might in one sense be said never to languish. 'You see,' said she to any friend who happened to be at hand, 'these editors are particularly kind to me. They always make a point of answering me themselves, and they never fail to use a nice adjective when speaking of my poor little efforts to express my thoughts. If they chose to be disagreeable, they might take no notice at all of me, but somehow when they write they seem to write so gratefully. It's the next best thing to being a successful author, to have so many of these nice kind refusals !'

Having so many friends among the literary classes, Miss Everilda was quite delighted when a friend of hers, who had married an eminent publisher, asked her to a garden party on July 30, where she was sure to see not only authors, male and female, but those much more important persons the publishers, who can, by merely giving an order, advance battalions of type to help you to rule in the republic of letters. The garden party was to be followed by a dance, and Mrs. Kennedy gave her old friend permission to bring with her her two young cousins, Mary and Agnes Treherne ; for be it known to all who like to hear of instances of the wonders worked by woman's quiet influence, Miss Everilda had banished what she was pleased to designate the odious and unseemly appellations, 'Polly' and 'Aggy.' The elegant-minded Miss Everilda had completely triumphed over these two rough girls. When first she came to Lorne Gardens it had been quite on the cards that they would act on the impression that their mother's cousin had been sent with a special eye to their amusement. But Miss Everilda was kind. She pitied them for being so ill-dressed and looking so awkward, and being rich, did not content herself with pity, but paid for dancing lessons for them, discovered that they had good voices, and gave them singing lessons, and bought them some pretty dresses. Of course the old Polly and Aggy were not entirely exterminated, that would have been impossible, but their worst vulgarities were banished, and a fine coat of varnish was put over the rest. If Miss Everilda had heard any of the doubtful expressions of other days they would have pained her inexpressibly; but she never did, and never so much as suspected to what depths her young cousins had erewhile descended. The Kennedys lived in St. John's Wood. Their house stood in a large garden. It was a half-wild garden, with a few fine trees standing in a tangled mass of ivy, and there were banks of ferns which the Kennedys were fain to persuade themselves were doing well in London, and had entirely forgotten that only a year ago they had been feasting on fresh air and revelling in damp in a lovely Devonshire lane. They looked very well in the garden at Green Bank, for the abundant stock of life and health they had brought up to town with them was still sufficient to supply them with vigorous new fronds. It was a very pretty garden, with a large lawn in the centre and broad walks all round it, over-shadowed by trees. When the Trehernes entered with Miss Everilda, the lawn was covered with people who were standing in little groups, talking or silently watching a very well-played game of tennis. Agnes had never been to an entertainment of the kind before, and her surprise was so great that she exclaimed, 'Oh, my dear Miss Everilda, what a number of delightful-looking people!'

'Indeed there are,' said Miss Everilda. 'Oh, here is Louisa—Mrs. Kennedy, I mean. How are you? How kind you are to let me bring my young cousins! Don't forget, my dear Louisa, that though I am a frequent correspondent of several of your literary friends, I don't know any of them by sight. Is the editor of the " Abstract Hour" here? Do introduce me to him if he is, and I should like to be introduced to the editor of " Culture" too. He has been so kind to me, he has written me such nice encouraging letters —at least, he has gone far towards turning the cold formal notice they send out, into letters, by his pleasant and complimentary choice of words.'

' They are both here somewhere, I saw them

five minutes ago. Oh, that is Mr. Forester, standing by the fountain with—I don't know who is with him ; they are watching the tennis.'

'Watching the tennis! Well, I suppose he must unbend sometimes,' said Miss Everilda discontentedly. She thought it was unworthy of a denizen of the heights of literature to watch tennis.

'He is generally unbent when I see him. Come and be introduced. By-the-bye, Everilda, if I were you, I don't think I would mention having corresponded with him.'

'Oh, but I must. It would be most ungrateful not ; besides, it seems kinder to spare him the trouble of racking his memory about me ; he is sure to remember my poem, but may have partly forgotten my name. Introduce me, dear, do.' And the poor little lady looked at her friend's face in eager anxiety to know if this crisis in her fate were actually close at hand or not. Her manner was so nervous and her gaze so appealing, that Mrs.

Kennedy could not but feel pity for this upper-class member of the great body of the unemployed. 'Come, dear,' said she, and began to move slowly towards Mr. Forester, but she stopped on the way to introduce Mary and Agnes to some nieces of hers. Then they walked on towards the fountain; but halfway there Mary exclaimed, 'Agnes, just look, do look, there is John Simonds; how nice he looks, but how ill!'

'Oh, please do not stop now,' said Miss Everilda; 'do let me go with Mrs. Kennedy now while she can stay with me, it is so important. We can go and speak to your friend afterwards.' So they hurried on, and the introduction was performed. For one moment Miss Everilda gazed on Mr. Forester as if the rugged steeps of Mount Parnassus had suddenly been smoothed and laid down with soft green turf for her weary feet; then she said in a low and nervous voice, 'I have so wished to be introduced to you.' He bowed and looked down in surprise on the fair-complexioned, blue-eyed, good-looking lady, dressed in delicate grey, who seemed to attach so much importance to possessing his acquaintance. She was so obviously in earnest, and her manner was so timidly eager, that though, man-like, he felt a burning desire to get away from what promised to be a conversation of an unusual kind, he still felt interest and a certain unaccountable pity.

'It was so very kind of you to send me those few words of encouragement—about my " String of Pearls," you know.'

Mrs. Kennedy saw that Mr. Forester had not the least idea what Miss Everilda meant, and said in a low voice, ' Something Miss Seaton sent you for the magazine, I think ; ' then her attention was claimed by some one else, and John Simonds had come up to speak to Mary and Agnes, so Mr. Forester was left with his tormentor.

' Yes,' said she, glad of the help Mrs. Kennedy had given her; ' a little poem I sent you.' (Untrained writers always talk of their poems; a poet contents himself with calling them verses.) 'I christened it "A String of Pearls," because, you see, it was rather like a string of pearls. I have the thoughts, but find it so difficult to give them expression; I am shy even with myself. I did somehow manage to utter some small part of what I was feeling, but not in the regular connected way that any one of a less timid and sealed-up nature could have done. So I gave the poem a title to show that I did not consider that I had achieved quite as much as I ought to have done. You did not accept it for your magazine, perhaps I ought not to have expected you to do so, but you wrote such a kind little word on the printed notice; without your name, of course, but I learnt that when I came here to-day.'

Mr. Forester looked bewildered; he remembered the poem, but he did not remember any special kindness in the refusal of it, or that he had any hand in it.

'It is only a fortnight ago, and you may

have forgotten the circumstance entirely, but I have not, and I thank you.'

'I am afraid you are thanking me for very little,' said he, bowing and preparing to move away. He did remember the 'poem' in question, but only because of the very odd note which had accompanied it. He had read that first, and had then turned to look at 'The String of Pearls.' He had found the string easily enough, but had never succeeded in finding the pearls, and had declined the contribution with the editor's compliments and many thanks, and that was all. He got away as soon as he could, and later in the afternoon, as he went home with the editor of 'Culture,' the two compared notes. The latter had had the offer of 'The Cry of the Wayside Dove,' by the same pen, which he had not thought pertinent, and had declined in polite terms, but had happily escaped the writer's gratitude.

'Oh, John, who would have thought of our seeing you here?' Mary had exclaimed when she saw John Simonds by her side.

'Why not, Polly?' he asked.

'Hush!' said Mary anxiously. 'Don't say Polly now; you really must not!'

'I beg your pardon,' said John sadly: 'do forgive me. I know I ought not to be so intimate now, but it is so difficult to break myself of the old habit.'

'Oh, John, it is not that at all! Why should you not be just the same with us as you have always been? It is only that we have dropped a great many careless ways of talking. A cousin of my mother's is staying with us who is quite a distinguished authoress; you don't know what a quantity of beautiful poems she has written! They make a pile quite a quarter of a yard high, and all good; and she has spoken to us about some of our words and ways, and taken a great deal of pains with our looks and our manners, and now we always say Mary and Agnes, and never use those ugly short names—do we, Aggy?' This slip of poor backsliding Polly's broke the ice effectually, and John, who had looked very grave and reserved when he first joined them, was soon nearly as much at home with them as ever.

'Have you given up calling your other sister by her short name too?' he asked. He could not altogether shake off reserve when speaking of her.

'Zeph, you mean; no, we are to go on giving her the same name we have always done, Miss Everilda says, because there is something original about it. She says that names beginning with Z are so uncommon that they are quite distinguished. Miss Everilda—Miss Seaton, I mean—lives near Alnminster, John; have you heard of her?'

He had just heard of her; and then they asked him how he liked Alnminster. He liked it, he said, but he did not like being so far away from every one. Then he said rather shyly, 'Are you alone here? I mean is your sister with you?'

'No,' replied Mary, 'Zeph has been staying at Berkhampstead Castle since the beginning of June.'

' I might have guessed it,' said he, looking very much downcast.

' You need not think that she is there for any reason of the kind you seem to be imagining,' said Mary impetuously. 'She is only there because father and mother are. Mr. Daylesford asked father to go and arrange all the MSS. at the castle for him, and gave him a very good salary for doing it; I am sure you will be glad to hear that. Zeph and mother were asked to stay there with father as long as they liked; but you must not think that Mr. Daylesford himself has been with them, for he has not. He has only been at the castle for two days, or perhaps three, ever since they first went.'

' Is that a fact? '

' Of course it is. He has been all the way to the Icarian Islands to see his brother, and since he came back he has stayed in London —he has not been with them in the country at all. That is true, John, I assure you. We ourselves saw him when he first came home;

and besides, Zeph would have told us if he had been there.'

' When did you last hear from her?'

' Three or four days ago, and she said they were quite alone.'

John sighed, and then he looked at Mary as if he would like to ask her something.

' John,' said she, with a sudden desire to try to make him look happier; ' you look as if you would like to ask me something, and there is a great deal I should like to say to you.'

John glanced at the crowd. What man ever does forget the presence of his fellow-creatures; not even when a few words which it is most important that he should hear could be said quite safely? Polly looked to see what Miss Everilda was doing. She was talking of the wrongs of authors with a sister in the craft to whom she had just been introduced by Mrs. Kennedy, and with whom she would evidently be content to stay for hours. Agnes was talking to a good-looking young figure-painter who was longing to ask her to sit for Gudrun.

'They are all happy,' said Mary to John Simonds. 'Let us walk round the garden. We can talk there, and I have something to say to you.' They strolled to the shady path under the elm trees, she wondering much at her own audacity the while. How had she dared to say this to him, and what more was she going to say when they reached the spot where they would be comparatively alone? She had been distressed by the sight of his evident unhappiness, and she could not but remember the time when they were all young together, and how, even then, he had loved Zeph. She respected his constancy with all the respect of a person who was not at all sure that she herself could ever attain to any proficiency in that virtue. He had been such a dear amusing fellow in those old days, and so upright and honourable, that if he said a thing was wrong, she and her sisters felt at once that it must not be done. Now he was manifestly suffering great depression on Zeph's account, and part of it Mary thought was caused by the consciousness that Zeph had behaved in a way that was unworthy of her. 'John,' she said very earnestly, 'you must be surprised at my asking you to come and talk to me. Promise me, even if you are vexed with anything I may say, to believe I spoke with a good motive.'

'I can promise that quite easily,' said he. 'I know you are acting from the best of motives—I can see that you are.'

'Thank you,' replied Mary gently. 'You make it easy for me to speak. What I want to say is this: I think you are blaming my poor sister very much in your own mind for her conduct to you—I won't pretend that I do not know what has happened, for I cannot help knowing it—but if you think that she behaved as she did because she preferred another and a richer man, I honestly assure you you are wrong.'

He looked at her, and there was something in his eyes which showed a struggle to believe her, but a strong feeling that she must be mistaken.

' Don't look as if you could not believe me, John ; it is perfectly true. I ought not to tell Zeph's secrets—indeed, I know none that I have not discovered for myself—but I am sure, absolutely sure, that if she loves any one, it is you ! '

He shook his head gloomily, but she saw that he walked more lightly, and she took it as a sign that he was beginning to have a little more belief.

' But, Polly,' he urged, wholly oblivious of her late remonstrance, ' if that be the case why did she refuse me ? '

' Zeph is odd in many ways,' answered Polly. ' She is naturally much more refined than any of us. She likes everything to look pretty and go smoothly, and has endured so many of what she calls the rubs of poverty, that she will never, of her own free will, marry a poor man. Excuse my seeming to call you a poor man, John.'

' Oh, I am poor, there is no denying that ; but I shall not always be poor, Polly. I mean to work ; and even as I am, I almost think that she and I would be better off than she is at home.'

'Yes, but at home she does not feel responsible for what she has to bear—she dislikes it, but she did not choose her lot, and if she were to marry you, it would be choosing a certain way of life with her eyes open.　I know she thinks that : I have heard her say things from time to time, and have pieced her opinions together.'

'If those are her opinions she cannot love me ! ' said John, as if all were definitely over.

'I am perfectly certain she does, and that she is very unhappy because she has refused you.'

'Impossible ! '

'Not impossible at all !　I am convinced that I am giving you a faithful idea of what she feels.'

'If she loved me she would be content to run the risk of having to bear a few years of comparative poverty with me.　She would wish to do so, in fact, for she would hope to make it easier to me. Do you mean to say, Polly, that if you loved any man in my position, you would shrink from marrying him from the motives you assign to your sister ? '

Polly blushed from the roots of her hair to the tips of her fingers—John had never seen such a sudden blush before. She struggled to answer, and said, ' I would not, but Zeph would.'

' And yet you say that Zeph loves me.'

' And yet I say that Zeph loves you,' repeated Polly mechanically. She was feeling shyer than she had ever felt in her life, and terribly afraid that she was playing the part of a traitor in revealing what she believed to be the true state of her sister's mind. Something she could not account for had made her speak. She knew what Zeph was suffering, and she had only to look at John to see what Zeph's decision had cost him. Why should these two people go on being wretched if she could conquer her dislike to speak to him, and by telling him the honest truth bring them together?

He was hard to persuade, principally because he did so wish to be persuaded. 'It cannot be true, Polly,' said he; 'you are a dear kind girl, but you are deceived. Zeph is much more likely to be in love with Mr. Daylesford than with me.'

'Oh, but I happen to know that she is not,' replied Polly stoutly.

He turned suddenly, and looked at her with such eager hope kindling in his eyes, that her heart ached at not having any further comfort to give him.

'That young gentleman is making an offer of marriage,' said a passer by, the moment he reached a safe distance.

'Is the girl going to take him?' asked the lady who was with him.

'I don't know; there are evidently rocks ahead. I would trust a great deal to her power of moulding circumstances. She is a fine-looking creature—not a beauty, I don't mean that—and not quite of the upper class perhaps, but made of good stuff.'

' Oh, but he is a thousand times too good for her,' replied the lady ; ' he is really handsome and gentlemanlike, and she is—at least, I cannot help thinking she is—a little vulgar; she looks very like a shrew on her good behaviour.'

Their secluded path was therefore not quite secluded enough to prevent their encountering a little criticism now and then, but they dropped their voices, or were silent when any one approached ; and as for the criticism, they were unaware of it.

' You can solemnly affirm that it is your belief that there is nothing between your sister and Mr. Daylesford ? ' repeated John earnestly. ' Dear Polly, do not be so unkind as to say one word more than you can say with perfect certainty.'

Polly paused in order to answer this with greater conscientiousness. ' I sincerely think —no, I am perfectly certain—that there is no affection on her side : I cannot answer for his feelings.   I have only seen him once or twice, but I do not think that there is any sign of his being in love with her, unless it is his troubling himself to know us at all, and I think father's being of such use to him in arranging his MSS. would account for that.   They went to Berkhampstead in June—he went with them. When he had been there for two days, or perhaps three, he went away to the Icarian Islands, but if he had not gone there he was coming back to London that same day.   When he got to Paris he must have heard that his brother was safe, but he went on and he paid him a long visit; he was away for at least a month, and when he did come home he did not go to Berkhampstead to see her, and he had not had any letters from her, for he came to our house to ask if father and the others were still at the castle, and when we told him that they were, he did not go to them, for Jack saw him in Oxford Street.   Now, John, does what I have just told you convince you that there can be nothing between them? for it is my opinion it ought. Besides, is it likely that a man in Mr. Daylesford's position would condescend to marry Zeph?'

This was too much for John, he was in arms at once. 'Condescend to marry Zeph—I should think he, or any man, however high his position was, might feel it an honour and a privilege to win your sister's love! You say that he has not won it; can you give me equally good proof of that?'

'No, Zeph is reserved, and I am sorry to say she and I often have quarrels—she would never confide in me. She does not confide in Agnes either; it would be Jack if it were any one—Jack is the one she loves most, and he says she loves you, and I am certain she does; and as for her caring for Mr. Daylesford, do you think if she did that she would have said what she did to me when I was at Berkhampstead for the day?'

'What did she say? Polly, do excuse me, but it is life or death to me.'

'I asked when he was coming back, and

she said she hoped not at all while they were
at the castle, and that she was very glad he
had gone to his brother, and hoped he would
stay a long time. Then I asked if she would
like to see you.'

'What did she say to that?'

'She said nothing at all. We were walking
in the park, and she hurried away from the
path and stooped down to gather some flowers,
and I followed her, and when she got up again
I saw two great glassy tears standing in her
eyes, and knew that she had gone away to hide
them. I said, "Zeph dear, why don't you let
John come? half a word would bring him to
you wherever he was if you would but say it,
or let some one else say it for you." She put
her hand on my arm and said, "Hush, Polly!
don't talk of that, you make me so unhappy."
So I said no more, but you must see that it is
you whom she loves.' John turned very pale
and leaned against a tree by the edge of the
path ; he dared not let himself believe it, and
yet belief was trying to take possession of his

mind. Polly was silent; she had nothing more to say, but she looked at him with pitying kindness.

'What would you have me do?' said he hoarsely.

'My dear John!' said Polly, and there was something in her voice which showed her astonishment at his question. He looked up, wishing only that she would direct his conduct a little; his head was reeling at the sudden change of outlook.

'Why, go to her of course—go at once! I don't quite know how you have managed things, but so far as I can judge you must have said what you wanted to say to her at odd moments or by letter. You have never had a real talk with her—never! See her; say what you want to say by word of mouth! I am absolutely certain that if you do she will not be able to resist you, for her heart is on your side.'

'I will do it!' said he resolutely; 'I will go. God bless you, dear Polly, for the kindness you have shown me to-day. Whatever happens I shall never forget it—and it costs a girl an effort to speak as you have done.' This speech was an indication of one of the strongest points of John's character. Filled as his mind was with his own anxieties and newly born hopes which had not strength to soar, he could yet divert his mind from them and put himself in her position. He took her hand and held it in a warmly affectionate grasp, and the two who had observed them before caught sight of this action from afar, and said, 'She has accepted him!'

'My dear Mary,' said Miss Everilda to that young lady when she at last returned to her chaperon's side, 'I have had such a delightful conversation! This lady, Miss Lampeter—let me introduce my cousin to you, Miss Lampeter —knows much more about authorship than I do, and she has told me all kinds of things about getting poems and articles published that I never knew. I now see quite clearly why my poor poems have never been printed. It all comes of my disregarding the most trifling formality imaginable. I ought, when I sent one to this or that editor, to have always enclosed my visiting card as well. It does seem such a pity that I did not know this before. Some one should really have told me.'

Miss Everilda was so light-hearted, that if the editor of ' Culture ' had asked her to tread a measure with him she would infallibly have done it. Failing that, she watched the young people enjoying themselves, and she began a poem in which gaslight and moonlight were contrasted, and asked John Simonds to come and see her when they were back in the north again, and read some of her MS. poems. John hung about, waiting for the chance of a little more talk with Polly, but had to be content with such as could be had in odd moments between the dances. He was well content to wait her pleasure, for by a few words she had changed the aspect of the world to him.

CHAPTER XVIII.

THE AGONY COLUMN.

And I had rather have one twinkling,
  Child Waters, of thine ee,
Than I wolde have Cheshire and Lancashire both,
  To take them mine own to be.—*Ballad of Child Waters.*

UNTHINKING persons, Zeph Treherne among the number, were apt to maintain that Dr. Simonds was nothing more than a dry and most uninteresting old gentleman, whose conversation was so heavy that no dinner party could overcome the weight of his presence. There was truth in the assertion so far as concerned conversation on topics which did not interest him, and nothing did interest him heartily but matters concerning his own profession, or in some way allied with it. It was his religion, his poetry, his art. He had been heard to say that there was no sight in nature more beautiful than a perfectly healthy, healing sore ; but if he had an eye which admired wounds of this sort he had a heart to feel for mental wounds likewise. To the outside world he was a cold man—he was a perfect slave to his patients. He became so interested in them that if he had thought the recovery of one of them was ever so slightly retarded by the non-fulfilment of some wish, he would have gone miles to remove the difficulty if it were in his power to do so. He considered that he was under a solemn obligation to better the condition of all who entered the wards over which he presided, and beginning his ministrations in that spirit, he often ended in being all but a father to his patients, whose sorrows became his own. Dr. Simonds was physician to St. Elizabeth's Hospital, and for some time his thoughts had been much occupied with a patient who, some few weeks ago, had been brought into one of the private wards. She was a girl, Hester Langdale by name, and young. When she first came in she had been suffering from a brain attack presenting some features which

were unfamiliar to him. She had evidently
been placed in circumstances which had caused
her acute mental pain, most probably the de-
sertion of her lover ; but the result had been
that she was now the victim of a strange freak
of memory. There was nothing that had ever
been learnt, or read, or seen by her that did
not reproduce itself now. Whether it was a
long poem, or a psalm of David's, or a prayer,
she could repeat it with perfect accuracy, word
by word, and the lines followed each other
with as much ease as if she had been winding
off silk from a perfectly unentangled ball. Her
father had not been able to buy books for her,
and had therefore, even when she was still a
young child, made her learn by heart every
poem or fragment of poem that he himself admired, and these were torturing her now. Her
mind was strangely active in furnishing her with
opportunities of exercising this newly developed
power. Hardly had she completed the task of
going through one poem which had been stored
away for years in the limbo of long-forgotten

things than another line from another equally forgotten poem darted into her thoughts, and she was stimulated to try to recollect the next, and then the whole poem gradually unrolled itself before her mental vision, and she was able to repeat it to the very end. Then came the wish to know the beginning also, and to repeat it up to the very point at which memory had supplied the line which had started her off. She always seemed to feel a certain difficulty in remembering the first line, but no sooner did she do this—for she never failed to succeed in her attempts in a few minutes—than she was as familiar with it as she had been with the rest; and it was the same with conversations and scenes which had taken place almost in her babyhood; and thus she became aware of many a circumstance of which she had hitherto had no knowledge. The consequence of this most unnatural state had been that Hester was worn to a shadow. She hardly ever slept or rested, for her brain would not consent to let her have any repose. There was a terrible amount of grief and despair lurking behind all this triumphant recollection of bygone days and things, for she always seemed to triumph a little when she succeeded in repeating something she had learnt to please her father, who had died so long ago that his image was fading from her mind. Now his features were distinctly seen by her and his words to herself distinctly remembered, and that not with pain, but with a certain amount of pleasure. The pain came when she was going through some poem which Daylesford and she had enjoyed together. Then she burst into agonies of tears; and these attacks and her sleeplessness were what Dr. Simonds at first found it so hard to struggle with. He had done so with success; the over-excitement of brain which reproduced so many apparently extinct impressions had been relieved; but, strange to say, the recollections she had thus regained remained with her in all their freshness, but she was so weak that Dr. Simonds was often alarmed. Every day since she had first come to the hospital that she was able to speak at all, she had repeatedly asked for the 'Times' newspaper, and at first it had been given her in compliance with her most piteous entreaties. She had never looked beyond the first page, and had wept so after seeing it that her doctor had forbidden it to be brought to her any more. For some time she had said less about it; in fact, the period during which she had any reason to expect to see Daylesford's advertisement was over, and she knew it. Still she sometimes asked for the paper; but discipline was strict at St. Elizabeth's, and she was told that Dr. Simonds had forbidden it as seeing it only made her worse. 'Dr. Simonds is mistaken, he does not understand,' said Hester wearily.

'He ought to know, Miss—he is a doctor,' said the nurse, shocked at such language.

'I shall ask him this morning,' said Hester, on the morning of the very day when the Trehernes went with Miss Everilda to the Kennedys' garden party. 'I am better, it won't do me any harm to-day,' she pleaded, when he had come and she was preferring her request. He looked at her pale face; how large her eyes looked now that she was so thin! she had no idea how ill she still was.

'Feel my pulse,' said she; 'look at me, and you will see for yourself how much better I am.' He saw that she was trying to seem stronger than she was for the sake of carrying her point, while even the energy with which she had said these few words had been too great a tax on her strength. She saw a denial framing itself on his lips, and turned her face away and began to weep quietly. 'Send for a copy of the " Times," nurse,' said he. 'There, you shall have your way for once, Miss Langdale. I wish you would tell me why you want it,' he added, when the woman had left them. 'I am an old man, you need not mind confiding in me; I might be of service to you, my poor dear child.'

'Yes, you are kind,' murmured Hester, ' very kind. It was you who made them put my hair where I can see that it is safe.' They both glanced at a shining roll of hair which was tied by a ribbon to a nail in the wall by the side of Hester's little white bed. During the worst part of her illness he had ordered her hair to be cut off, and she, who had then been so weak and ill as to be careless about preserving her habit of reticence, had said, 'I must have that hair kept. If Godfrey ever sends for me to go back to him, he will be vexed with me for letting my hair be cut off!'

'Who is Godfrey, and where is he?' the doctor had then asked, but she had shaken her head in tearful silence.

'You are getting a little better,' said he. 'Do you feel the improvement yourself?'

'I don't know,' she replied gloomily; 'I am not sure that I want to be better. Oh, that is so ungrateful!' she exclaimed, for she remembered his constant kindness. 'Yes, I feel better—much better.'

'Your "Times" will be here in a minute,' said he. 'Promise me, if you do not find what you want in it, not to make yourself ill again with crying. That is what makes me so afraid of letting you have it. Do try to bear up.'

'You do not know what I have to bear up against,' she answered piteously, 'and it came on me so suddenly too! I hope I shall bear it better some day, and I will try to make that day come as soon as possible to please you.'

The nurse now came with the 'Times.' Hester at once turned to the second column of the first page, but no sooner did she look at it than her eyes fell on the four words for the sight of which she had hungered so long. ' Hester, you are wrong,' in large letters. She could scarcely believe her senses. It seemed so impossible that those words could really be there. Could it be true, and were her days of misery at an end? Then a bright but most delicate flush overspread her wan cheeks, and she looked into the doctor's face, her eyes blinded with happy tears. 'Look!' said she, and pointed to the words.

He saw them in a moment. 'There!' said

he triumphantly ; ' didn't I always tell you you were wrong ? '

' You did,' she answered gently, ' but you did not know what a terrible number of reasons I had for thinking myself right. I was so wretched when first it happened that I thought I must have drowned myself. I don't know how I escaped that. I don't know how long it is since it happened, for I have been so ill. He went away. He was to come back in four days and to write to me during the time, and he never wrote and never came, and from that day to this I have never heard one word from him.'

' But,' said the doctor anxiously, ' how can you be quite certain that this announcement is intended for you ? '

' Because when I left his house—I felt I ought to leave it—I wrote a line to say that I was going, but that supposing there had been some unfortunate mistake about his letters and he had written, and did not want me to leave him, he was to put a message to me consisting

of these four words in the " Times ; " and oh,
doctor, perhaps they have been in every day
for a long time.　You have never allowed me
to see a paper.　I don't want to say anything
unkind to you, but how could you refuse me
that ?　I might have been happy all the time.'

'I did it for the best,' said he.　'I was only
thinking of your health.'

'I know you were,' said she warmly ; 'but
now I must go.　I must go at once.'

'Impossible !　You are not able.　It is as
much as your life is worth to attempt it.'

'I must ; I will rest when I am there.'

' But how far is it ? ' asked Dr. Simonds, for
in spite of himself he wavered for one moment.

'You must not ask that ; but it won't hurt
me—it's not far.'

'I cannot give my consent,' said he, recovering his firmness.　'The risk is much too
great ; and you must compose yourself and not
talk any more.　I am afraid you will suffer for
this ; I shall have to administer a sedative.'

'How can I compose myself when I have

seen that announcement? How can I stay here when I might be with him? Doctor, you are kind and good, and you have saved my life I know; but now that I am so much better, one word from him will do more for me than all the medicine and care in the world.'

'Listen,' said he authoritatively. 'It is absolutely impossible for you to leave this place for some days, perhaps not for a week.'

'A week,' she began; but he interrupted her.

'Let me finish what I was saying. And you must be absolutely quiet.'

'Quiet! You forget what is in that paper. I must answer it. I must see him. You must let me go!'

'In a day or two,' he said firmly.

'In an hour! Think how many hours of being together have already been lost! You forget that he is unhappy too. I should be un-worthy of his affection if I let him suffer one half-hour's unhappiness that I can spare him.'

The doctor looked embarrassed. He was a

quiet, God-fearing man, who liked people to be bound by the ordinary rules of Christian morality. He could see that she wore no wedding ring; every word she said proved that she was no wife; he shrank back from his own desire to offer to do something to help her. How could he be the go-between in an affair of that kind? 'My dear child,' said he, 'I pity you from the bottom of my heart; but ought you to go back to him? Perhaps God has parted you from him for your own true good.'

'If God did that,' said Hester humbly, 'He will guide the rest until He shows His will. Let me do what I think best.'

'Well, so far as to-day is concerned, at the very most I can only allow you to write to him. Write and say where you are, and ask him to come perhaps, and I will send your note by my coachman. He can drive there, wherever it is, as you say it is so near, and still be back here before I am ready to go. I have other patients to see.'

The nurse's eyes seemed to say, 'Indeed

you have, sir;' but she knew his ways. Hester's beamed with happiness; that did seem such a quick method of communicating with Daylesford; but when a pen was put in her hand she found out how weak she was, and at first it seemed as if she would not be able to form a legible word. They had given her a sheet of note-paper with the hospital address printed on it, so all that she really needed to write was 'Godfrey, I am here; come,' and sign her name. That is what she did write, but in such trembling characters that she feared it would be impossible for him to read it.

'Doctor,' said she anxiously, 'I shall have to ask you to be so kind as address this for me. I dare not trust my own writing. You will keep my secret?'

He bowed, and silently took the pen and wrote, The Hon. Godfrey Daylesford, 11 Ambassadors' Gate. Again he felt that there was some story connected with that name; he was sure he had heard it before, but could not say when or where.   He was a very absent and oblivious man; but Hester did not know it, or she would not have lain back on her pillow now with such a happy smile on her lips.   He bade her farewell for the day, intending at once to send off his man with her note; but in the corridor he was waylaid by the house surgeon, who had been wishing for some time that he would deal more expeditiously with that case in Private Ward Number 4. A poor man, in whom Dr. Simonds had quite as much interest as in Hester Langdale when once he was in sight of his evident suffering, was anxiously waiting for his visit, and an important change had taken place in his symptoms; so, without having the least idea what he was doing, the doctor put the note in his pocket and hurried to the patient whom he had neglected too long. Then he had to see another and yet another. He did not remember what he had left undone until more than an hour afterwards, when he was descending the hospital steps and saw his own coachman. Then he bethought himself of the errand which he had promised to entrust to this man.

'I have lost more than an hour,' he thought; 'and that unhappy girl will be lying there counting every second! Eleven Ambassadors' Gate,' said he, getting into his carriage as quickly as he could. He would deliver the letter with his own hands at Mr. Daylesford's door, and thus do his best to atone for his culpable forgetfulness. He soon reached his destination, and jumped out with professional promptitude. As soon as the footman saw him he bowed and said, ' Please to walk in, sir; you are expected.'

What was this? Had Hester after his departure written another letter to say that he would call? But she could not have done so, for his going there was a pure accident, and she had no reason to expect him to do it. The doctor was bewildered, hopelessly bewildered and undecided, and stood at the door not knowing what to do.

' Please to walk in, sir; you are expected,'

again said the footman, and there was so much
decision, not to say compulsion in his manner,
that Dr. Simonds made a few steps forwards
and immediately found the house door shut
behind him.   Perhaps it would not be amiss if
he did see this Mr. Daylesford, as he could not
only put the note into his own hands, but give
him an urgent warning not to let his patient talk
much or think of moving until she was actually
convalescent.   This idea gradually shaped itself,
but he was not quite sure whether it would not
be taking too great a liberty if he were to act
on it.   He meditated on this point as he followed the footman through the hall and corridor to the library. 'What a handsome house!'
thought he.   'Mr. Daylesford is rich, that's
very certain.   It is stupid of me to forget what
I have heard about him.   I don't think I have
ever met him, but I shall know that directly I
see his face.'

Dr. Simonds was not destined to see his
face that day ; the door opened and Mrs. Mason
bustled in, looking very important and full of

business. 'We have been expecting you, sir,' said she. A feeling of expectation seemed to have established itself in the mind of every one in the house. 'Mr. Daylesford said you would call,' she added.

'I am sure I don't know how Mr. Daylesford could expect me to——' began Dr. Simonds in ponderous amazement.

'No, nor I either,' interrupted Mrs. Mason. 'If he wants things to go right, he really ought to come himself and get the young lady to come, and then things could be arranged as they ought to be.'

'Oh, I should oppose that! I could not think of allowing her to come here——' interposed Dr. Simonds.

'But I should have thought you would have been very glad to have her here, and have some of the responsibility taken off you, sir.'

'I am accustomed to responsibility,' replied Dr. Simonds in his best professional manner, and with an admirably haughty bow.

'Well, you must be,' said Mrs. Mason, who was for a minute or two considerably impressed by his lofty manner, but the remembrance of certain bills enabled her to recover herself quickly, and she added, 'And then, you see, the high prices you charge go to cover that.'

'I am not aware that my prices are higher than is usual in the profession—they are not so high as those of many practitioners.'

'Perhaps not,' said Mrs. Mason doubtfully; 'but had we not better go over the house and settle what is to be done for the young lady's reception? I shall have left Mr. Daylesford's service before she comes, but I should like to do all I can for him.'

'But so little is needed—no great preparations for her reception are wanted; I will tell you anything I can think of. I should like to see Mr. Daylesford; I must say a word or two to him about her if you will kindly let him know I am here.'

'He is not here, sir; I thought I had explained that,' replied the disturbed housekeeper. 'Do let us just take a look round for you to form an opinion of what will be wanted. You say it will be very little. That's what Mr. Daylesford himself thinks; he says the house was put in thorough order a short while since when he took it, and all that he now wishes is that you should say what is absolutely necessary. He is intending to go abroad for three or four months very soon after his marriage, and he and his bride will only be here for a fortnight or so before they set off, even if they come at all.'

Dr. Simonds had heard nothing of this speech but the bit about Mr. Daylesford's marriage; his joy on hearing this was so great that he had thought of nothing else. It was a thousand times better than he had dared to hope. 'I am heartily glad he intends to marry her,' he said.

Mrs. Mason was beginning to be impatient. She liked to be treated as if she were a person of some importance, and she did not care to waste so much time on an old gentleman whose

principal occupation seemed to be wool-gather-
ing.   'Are you intending to examine into the
state of the house or not, if you please, sir ?'
said she.

'I presume that you mean from a sanitary
point of view?'

'Yes, that is one thing that has to be seen
to, but then there's a suite of rooms upstairs
that has to be re-decorated.'

'I don't see what I have to do with decora-
tion,' observed Dr. Simonds, who was more and
more at a loss to understand her.   'Madam, it
has struck me ever since I came in that we
were more or less at cross purposes, and excuse
me, my time is valuable.'

'That's what I have been thinking, sir.   Before more time is wasted, may I ask if you are
Mr. Waddilove, the upholsterer and decorator?
My master told me that I was to expect him
this afternoon, about doing up the suite of rooms
upstairs, and to see what more was needful.'

'Doing up a suite of rooms—decorations!
I am a doctor, madam, and I came here about

an announcement, which as I am informed was put in the "Times" newspaper by Mr. Daylesford. I must know where he is to be found—I must be able to take back some message to the lady to whom it was addressed! I have a note for him; how am I to send it?'

'I beg your pardon, sir. Mr. Daylesford is at present at the family's country seat. A letter will be sure to find him if you direct it to him at the castle. Berkhampstead Castle, sir.'

Dr. Simonds started and turned a shade or two paler. Now he knew who Mr. Daylesford was. He had heard his name more than once, some months ago, and never without much bitter comment. That was when Mrs. Simonds was most enraged against Zeph. Latterly all mention of her had been avoided as stirring up thoughts full of nothing but sorrow and pain, and in the whirl of professional life Daylesford's name had slipped out of the keeping of the doctor's memory. All that he had retained was that there was some man of fashion who had, as his wife maintained, turned Zeph's head by his unmeaning attentions. But the name of Berkhampstead brought everything back to his mind, and brought a dread of new sorrow as well. Up to the moment when the housekeeper uttered that name the doctor had not felt the smallest shade of doubt that Daylesford's undivided love was Hester's. How could he have had any anxiety on that point? How could any honest man have any? Had not the doctor seen an announcement in that day's 'Times,' put in by Daylesford himself, which according to agreement with Hester was not to appear unless he still loved and wished to be reunited to her? How could a man who had let that advertisement be printed, be about to marry any one but the woman to whom it was addressed? Now the doctor's heart was filled with an acute sense of danger and alarm. Zeph Treherne was, as he believed, at Berkhampstead Castle; Daylesford was there also. A marriage between these two would break the hearts of two far nobler creatures than themselves, and judging by the course of events in this wicked world, that seemed precisely the reason why such a marriage should take place.

'Shall I write down Mr. Daylesford's address for you, sir?' inquired Mrs. Mason, for he seemed quite indifferent to her presence, and was simply standing in a state of bewildered disquietude.

She recalled him to his senses, and he said, 'Oh no, there is no fear of my forgetting it;' and then, fumbling with his hat, and with a faint hope that she might contradict him, but more than all with a conviction that it was his bounden duty to obtain certainty, he added, 'Berkhampstead Castle, you said. Is not that where Mr. and Mrs. Treherne and some of their family have been staying?'

'They are staying there now, sir. It is the oldest Miss Treherne, you know, whom Mr. Daylesford is going to marry. It is quite a recent engagement. We only heard of it this morning.'

'But is it really an engagement? Do you

know for a fact that he is going to marry her, or are you merely supposing he intends it because he has been paying her some attention?'

'Well, I do think it begins to look uncommonly like a marriage when my master writes himself to tell me that he is going to be married, and that Mr. Waddilove will call to make some arrangements for the reception of his bride. None of us know the lady, I think I understood you to say you did?' and she fixed a piercingly interrogative eye on the doctor.

'What is your Mr. Daylesford's Christian name, madam?' asked the doctor, ignoring her curiosity entirely, for a sudden thought had come into his mind which had set his heart beating with renewed hope; there must be two brothers.

'His name is Godfrey; Mr. Godfrey Daylesford; and he might be Lord Berkhampstead if he would but consent to assume the title; and the young lady is said to be of good family too, and one of the most——'

'Don't speak of her!' exclaimed the doctor with loathing. 'Good morning, madam,' and he began to hurry out of the room.

'You think you can manage to recollect the address I gave you?' inquired Mrs. Mason, for to her mind he did not seem competent to put his own hat on his head. 'You won't forget Berkhampstead Castle?'

'Not till my dying day!' said he between his teeth, and thus left the house. But what was he to do? His spirit quailed when he thought of what lay before him. He would have to break this terrible news to the poor girl whom he had left lying at the hospital, supremely happy because the man she loved was still true to her, and having taken from her the only thing in the world for which she cared to live, he would have to go home and blight the existence of his best beloved son.

CHAPTER XIX.

THIS WAS SUCH PLAIN SPEAKING.

> Pray, pray, pray—no help but prayer,
> A breath that fleets beyond this iron world,
> And touches Him that made it.—TENNYSON.

LET no one accuse Dr. Simonds of cowardice because he went home instead of going back to the hospital to tell the worst to Hester. He told himself that he was not quite sure that the housekeeper's news was true, and that even if it were, his patient would bear it better if fortified by a night's rest after the excitement of the morning. That was the rock on which he took his stand, but let him look where he would, he saw no other rocks to stand on. He went to his own room and wrote a hasty note to Hester to tell her that Mr. Daylesford was out of town, but that he would forward her note to him. Then he wrote thus to Mr. Daylesford :—' I am physician to St. Elizabeth's Hospital, and Miss Hester Langdale is at present a patient in one of the private wards under my care. She has asked me to convey the enclosed letter or note to you, in answer, I believe, to an advertisement of yours in the " Times." I do so, but, for her sake and without her knowledge, I must add a line to say that, as her health is in a very critical state, I must entreat you to use the greatest circumspection in your dealings with her ; any abrupt or painful disclosure or communication might be highly injurious, if not fatal, in her present condition.'

' I ought not to have written this,' thought the doctor, ' but I'll take the breach of etiquette on my own conscience.' He wondered what Daylesford would do. The housekeeper had said that his engagement was quite a recent affair ; suppose it had been entered into under the impression that Hester was dead, or lost for ever. He would not have advertised in the

'Times' if he had not wished to find her; perhaps he had intended to make her his wife. When the note went to Berkhampstead, he would know that she was found. He would then be obliged to make his choice between the two women. If his choice fell on Hester, the renewal of love would probably end in a marriage, and if it did not fall on Hester, the doctor feared that he himself had perhaps been the cause of her unhappiness. He had refused her the sight of the 'Times.' He had done so because it always made her ill to see it. But would it have made her ill if she had found in it what she wanted? Had Daylesford's message to her been in the paper during the time when he had kept it out of her hands? and if so, was he, the doctor, answerable for the loss of her happiness? He could not forget that the housekeeper had said that the engagement was an affair of the last two or three days. If Hester had seen the advertisement sooner this fatal engagement might never have taken place, and Daylesford might have married her. He sent for the back numbers of the 'Times;' his wife kept such things, so there was no difficulty in finding them. He picked out all the supplements for the last three weeks, growing more and more despondent as he did so, for that announcement was in large print, and always caught his eye as readily as the name of the paper. Before long he was sitting, looking perfectly woebegone, with twelve supplements on his knee, every one of which contained the words, 'Hester, you are wrong!' They had first appeared on the 17th, and they had been in every paper since, ending with that very day, July 30th. And not one of these but the last had Hester been allowed to see! He was wretched.

After some time had passed, Mrs. Simonds looked in, and seeing him absorbed in thought —a state which she always described as sitting still and doing nothing—exclaimed, 'Well, my dear, you seem to be pretty well tired out.'

'Yes, dear, I am tired; I have had an exhausting day.' The doctor had no intention of increasing his many difficulties by telling her about Zeph, but he did want a little sympathy.

' I am sorry you are so tired, Ralph, but you do take your work far too much to heart. When you come home you ought to dismiss your patients from your mind—other doctors do. What's the use of fretting yourself to fiddle-strings about other people's troubles? and I am sure, at the rate you are paid for your hospital work, you can hardly be expected to give much thought to the cases when once you have turned your back on the building.'

He smiled, but very drearily, and said, ' I shall be all right presently. Where is John ? '

' At a garden party at St. John's Wood.'

Dr. Simonds sighed.

' Now why should you sigh because John is at a garden party at St. John's Wood? It is not as if you had to go.' But even that immunity brought the doctor no peace.

At dinner he tried to eat and speak, but in the evening he relapsed into silence again.

'My love,' observed Mrs. Simonds, ' no one can say that you are cheerful company.'

'I am afraid not,' he answered ruefully; ' but I have such a difficult matter to think about.'

' Let me help you,' she pleaded.

She was so wonderfully sympathetic that he forgot how rigidly severe her judgment was on certain points, and said, ' It's about a poor girl in the hospital who is just recovering from a brain attack, and who has been very cruelly treated by her lover.'

Mrs. Simonds was up in arms in a moment, and exclaimed, ' Dr. Simonds, you surprise me. Why should you trouble yourself about such a person? A girl in the hospital! What kind of a girl?'

' A very interesting one, but she has been most unfortunate. Her story is so sad.'

' Is she a respectable person?'

The doctor was sorely put to it—the question was so direct.

' No, not what you would call so, but she
is——'

' My dear, I hope your ideas on these points
are not getting confused with seeing so many
queer people.'

' Oh no, not that ; but if you did but know
how distressing it is——'

' Oh, I know the kind of people you go and
get unhappy about ! Whenever you see any
who are utterly good-for-nothing and useless—
so bad that no one else would look at them
—you go and pity them all the more because
you know no one else does, and then you worry
your life out in trying to do some very difficult
thing which will set them on their feet again.'

' My dear, I don't deserve such a high
character ; I should be proud indeed if I could
set on his feet one poor creature whom every
one else had left lying as a desperate case.'

' Well, you may feel like that if you choose,
but I call it feeling very like a fool ! Any one
knows people of that kind cannot really be set
on their legs—they stand up while you hold

them, or while it amuses them to let you think you can hold them, and then they just drop down again, and laugh at you.'

'Never mind that, Eliza, if you know that you have done your best.'

'Oh, but the more I have done, the more angry I am when it comes to nothing. It is far better to give them no chance of laughing at you.'

'——And never try to do a good action,' replied the doctor languidly; he was again thinking—there were so many things to think about; and now, having satisfied himself that he had done all in his power to lighten Hester's sufferings, he felt at liberty to torment himself with another aspect of the same affair, and one which touched him much more closely. How would his son bear the intelligence?

John came in very soon after the doctor had decided that there was no reason why he too should not be allowed to have one more night's rest unconscious of new sorrow. John looked twice as happy as when he went out, and Mrs. Simonds saw it, and raised her eyes from her knitting with a genuine touch of kindliness in them. 'How bright you look!' said she. 'Who was at the Kennedys? Any one you knew?'

'Yes, the Trehernes were there,' he replied joyously.

'Not Zeph, surely?' asked the doctor eagerly.

'No, not Zeph, but the two others. They have grown into such fine handsome girls!'

Mrs. Simonds muttered something very disparaging, and her rugged brow clouded over; then she said, 'Surely we have had enough, and more than enough, of these people! Their presence cannot have added much to your pleasure, John.'

'It did—I was very glad to see them again.'

'Oh, I think I will say good night,' she observed severely. 'I don't care to sit up to hear the praises of people I detest; and I like people to be consistent, and you are not. One of them has done all she could to make us miserable, and now these two younger ones seem to want to try to do the same. Leave them alone, John; they are as heartless as their sister, I make no doubt.'

During this speech both John and his father had been endeavouring to soothe her. 'Let us talk of something else, dear,' the doctor had said.

'Don't go away, mother,' exclaimed John; but she would listen to no entreaties, and went. She had not been gone a minute, however, before she opened the door again for one last attack on the Trehernes.

'They are a thoroughly worthless family, I tell you, and, for my part, I greatly wonder how you can condescend to speak to any of them—so now you have my opinion!' Having said this, she retreated without giving him time for an answer, and then John told his father all Polly had said to him, and that he was going to see Zeph next day. The doctor was rather silent, but, on the whole, hopeful, for if

Zeph had been engaged, surely Polly would have known it. Next morning the doctor meant to tell his son what he had heard at Ambassadors' Gate—that night he should sleep unvexed by doubt. As for the doctor himself, he was too much perplexed to sleep, and yet he had to pretend to be fast bound in its thrall, for if he moved or gave his wife the least opening to suspect that he was awake, she broke the welcome silence by some such speech as this :—

'Ralph, listen to me—you must listen to me. You may be lax about things—you always are! You may be willing to let those odious Trehernes play fast and loose with you and your family, but I give you warning—a solemn warning that I will never be civil to any one of them—none of them shall ever set foot in this house!' She rang changes on this the whole night long, the doctor always pretending to be too much under the dominion of sleep to take in the meaning of her words, and scarcely answering a syllable. But his night was so

disturbed that he overslept himself, and the
first thing he was conscious of in the morning
was his wife standing by his bedside, saying,
'It is too indecent! Such barefaced pursuit of
a young man is positively disgraceful!'

'What is the matter, my sweet Eliza?' he
asked, not in irony, but from imperfect com-
prehension of what was arousing him to play a
part once more in the troublesome world from
which he had for some hours escaped.

'That forward creature, Polly Treherne,
has actually sent that spoilt little brother of
hers here—here to this house, I tell you, Ralph
—with a note to John! She cannot even wait
till he has got his breakfast before she tries to
get hold of him again! Now, Ralph, John may
be what is called grown up, but I hope he is
not too much grown up to obey a kind father,
and I insist on your ordering him to keep away
from those scheming girls!'

The doctor was wide awake in a moment;
he greatly feared he knew why this note had
been sent. 'Let me get up and dress myself,'

said he; 'I will go to John.'   When he did go, John silently put into his hand Polly's note, which had evidently been written under the influence of strong feeling, and he read, 'Don't go to Berkhampstead to-day, John—don't go any day, for I have had a letter from my sister this morning.   All I told you yesterday was wrong, though, God knows, I thought I was telling you the truth : she is engaged to marry Mr. Daylesford.   I shall never forgive myself for causing you so much pain,'—(here it was easy to see that Polly had let one or two heavy tears fall on her paper)—'never.   And I am ashamed of her—she ought not to have done it.   Dear John, try to bear it bravely and forgive me.'

Dr. Simonds gazed blankly at his son, he was shocked at the anguish in his face.   Polly's letter had been a fearful blow to him after so many hours of hope.

'My dear boy,' said the doctor; but he himself looked as ill as his son.

'I shall bear it better in a short time,' said

John as cheerfully as he could. 'It has come on me rather unexpectedly, that's all. Don't tell my mother just yet.'

There could be no doubt now, and father and son went downstairs to face the world, which just then seemed inclined to treat them very hardly.

Mrs. Simonds was sitting at the breakfast-table looking full of just wrath, and pouring warm water in and out of the tea-cups with an air of consciousness that she was performing a service for two people who were miserably unworthy of any such kindness. Her face expressed a whole Commination Service.

'I suppose we had better begin,' said she coldly, looking from her anxious and unhappy husband to her equally unhappy son.

There was no satisfaction to be obtained from the face of either. If Dr. Simonds had carried his point and made John promise to have nothing more to do with the Trehernes; especially with this forward, giddy Polly, surely he would have seemed pleased. If, on the contrary, John had held his own, and maintained his right to keep on good terms with the friends of his youth, surely there would be some sign of firmness about him, if not of elation; but one seemed as depressed as the other. Breakfast was a silent and most uncomfortable meal. The two men rose up from it with a visible air of relief, and prepared to leave the room.

'Where are you going, Ralph?' inquired Mrs. Simonds imperatively.

'To the hospital.'

'My dear, it's not your day!'

'That's nothing! I shall have to go,' said the doctor resolutely.

'There are three or four people waiting for you downstairs—your own patients, you know —you will surely see them?'

Mrs. Simonds always affected to consider the hospital work as entirely outside of her husband's practice.

'Why was I not told before? I must go to

the hospital, of course, but it will do if I go rather later;' and as he looked glad of the respite, she was somewhat mollified.

'Here is a telegram for you,' said she, for the servant appeared with one. 'Now you will probably find some other work cut out for you than running to the hospital when you are not expected!'

'My dear Eliza,' he began; but he stopped, for who can check the torrent of a wife's eloquence?

He opened the telegram as he went downstairs, and when he saw who had sent it he was glad he had waited till then. It was from Godfrey Daylesford, Berkhampstead, and merely contained these words: 'Thank you for your caution. My lawyer will be with you at half-past twelve, to speak on the subject of your letter.'

Dr. Simonds went to his room and his patients, and Mrs. Simonds having, as she thought, her son at her mercy, said to him, 'Your father is going to waste his time at the hospital, and you, John, I suppose, are in a hurry to be off to the Trehernes?'

'Yes, mother, I am. I want to see Polly about something.'

Mrs. Simonds had not expected this answer. She had only been indulging in irony. When she heard it, she flung up her arms in horror at both father and son. Men were mad, unreasoning creatures at the very best, but surely she had become possessed of two of the worst specimens of their kind.

At two o'clock the doctor was on his way to the hospital. He had seen Mr. Daylesford's lawyer, who, as chance would have it, had been at Berkhampstead on business when the doctor's note enclosing Hester's had arrived. Daylesford had at once despatched him to London to see Dr. Simonds and explain his position. It was not a position to be proud of, and there was very little that the lawyer could say. Daylesford wished Hester to be informed that he had been abroad for a month or more, that he had written to her while away, that he had advertised for her, as requested in her last letter, as soon as he had received it, which he had not done till his return to England ; and besides that, he had made every possible inquiry ; but all being in vain, he had given up any hope of ever finding her, and had finally made an offer of marriage to a young lady to whom he had been for some time attached, but whose society he had avoided from a feeling of loyalty to Hester. Had he been able to find Hester he would, no doubt, have acted differently ; but as it was, his heart and his honour were alike pledged to another. Mr. Blackmore had wound up by saying that all that now remained for his client to do was to express his profound sorrow at having caused Miss Langdale any unhappiness, and his determination to settle an income of five hundred a year on her. The doctor had affirmed that he was quite certain she would not accept this. The lawyer had smiled faintly, and said he should be very much surprised if she did not. The doctor had said that many things that appeared surprising did nevertheless happen; for instance, some people might think it surprising that Mr. Daylesford, who was actually engaged to Miss Treherne, should put an announcement in the newspaper to inform Miss Langdale that his affection for her was unchanged, and yet that had actually happened.

'Oh, no, no!' exclaimed the lawyer, roused from his professional calmness by this attack. 'Let me explain that. Mr. Daylesford only proposed to Miss Treherne on the 28th; gentlemen do not usually attend to business at such times, but he wrote at once to stop that announcement appearing any more; but I suppose such things get set up in type earlier than we outsiders imagine—his letter was not in time to prevent it.'

'Mr. Daylesford seems to have been remarkably business-like!' observed the doctor bitterly. 'If he only became engaged to Miss Treherne on the 28th, he certainly lost no time in writing for an upholsterer and decorator to do his house up!'

'That also might be explained in a way not altogether to Mr. Daylesford's discredit,' said Mr. Blackmore. 'There was a suite of rooms in his house especially devoted to Miss Langdale's use, and the sight of them was painful to him.'

'I wonder what his feelings would be if he saw the poor girl herself?' said the doctor.

'But, Dr. Simonds, you must allow that my client is behaving as well as he can under the circumstances.'

'So much depends on the value people attach to money,' replied the doctor bitterly; 'I don't think Miss Langdale will care to receive any of his.'

'At all events you will let her know what Mr. Daylesford proposes,' said Mr. Blackmore.

'Some day I will, not yet. He may already be able to look on things from that point of view—I am certain that she is not—I doubt if she ever will be. Good morning, sir. People pity us doctors for having disagreeable work to do, but it seems to me that lawyers also are by

no means exempt from it. I will now go to
my patient, and will tell her as much of this as
I dare. I suppose I may infer that this is the
only reply to her note that Mr. Daylesford
intends to send ? '

'Precisely.'

'Then I wish you good morning, sir.'

The doctor had dismissed the lawyer hastily
and with ill-concealed contempt; but the contempt was principally directed against his
employer. He detested the idea of this man's
endeavouring to salve his own conscience by
offering a girl like Hester a money compensa-
tion. How could he who knew her insult her
so ? Meantime the doctor's hansom was rapidly
approaching St. Elizabeth's. The old man's
heart was very heavy. He did not think that
the blow would kill Hester, but he thought it
would tax her strength to the utmost.

'She has slept the whole night through,'
said the nurse; 'she looks much better, but she
is very anxious, sir.'

The doctor went in. Hester was lying

with her eyes fixed on the door, and she watched him enter the room. His head was slightly bowed. There was no brightness in his eyes, and they were not raised frankly to meet her own. He neither smiled cheerily as was his wont, nor were his lips set together like those of one who had a firm purpose— they expressed the anxious indecision of a man who has a painful duty to perform and has not been able to decide on any way of doing it. She drew the sheet over the lower part of her face as if she foresaw that ere long she would have need to hide the anguish that would be seen in it, and kept her eyes fixed on his. He came to the side of the bed, tried to speak, but his voice seemed thick ; then he took her hand and seemed more than ordinarily desirous to ascertain the true state of her pulse, but she felt that his hand was trembling.

'Tell me what it is, doctor,' said she, very gently. 'I know there is something that you are afraid to tell me—I see it—I feel it.'

He tried to gain time, for his courage failed

him, and he said, 'I hear that you have had a very good night.'

'Yes,' said she, 'a very good night. And yet I have heard nothing from him. You sent my letter?'

'Yes, I sent it.'

'Can there have been any mistake? He was away, you said, but you know he would get it this morning, and he might have sent a telegram just to make me happy.—Doctor!' she exclaimed suddenly, 'There are tears in your eyes!—You have bad news for me which you are afraid to tell?' He bowed his head in sign of assent—no man could have felt more wretched.

'He is going to be married?' said she, rushing at once to the furthest limit of her evil imaginings. He did not speak. She felt that he could not contradict her words. She lay perfectly still, but he could see a movement under the bed-clothes which revealed that she was clenching her hands together, and her face gradually assumed a rigidness which showed that she was bracing up her nerves to endurance. Two tears rolled down her ashy pale cheeks, but no others followed.

'Are you quite sure of this?' she at length asked in a very low voice. She spoke very slowly, but her voice was quite firm.

'My dear child, yes. I myself could not believe it at first, but unhappily it is true.'

'Why did he seem to want me back again, then? Why did he put that message to me in the paper?' said she, and each word she uttered seemed wrung from her only by a supreme effort of will.

'Don't think of it—don't think of him; his conduct is inexplicable.' The doctor and nurse both looked at their patient in the greatest apprehension—her face was growing more and more deathlike; but they could see that she was resolutely determined to endure to the end.

'Be as calm as you can, miss; you see you have your own health to think of,' urged the nurse, and she put out her hand to smooth away a bit of Hester's pretty brown hair from her forehead. She meant it more as an encouraging caress than a work of necessity, but at the last moment she shrank from doing it. Hester was far beyond reach of anything she could do to soothe her, and the nurse recognised the fact, and retreated.

'My dear,' said the doctor, 'Mr. Daylesford's housekeeper told me that this was quite a recent engagement. I shall always reproach myself for not letting you see those papers.'

The tears once more dimmed Hester's eyes. She put up her thin white hand to wipe them away, and hide a look of pain which was passing over her face.

'I am so grieved if you feel that I have done wrong about them,' said the poor old man.

'I don't. I don't think about that at all. I don't think about anything but him and all that I have lost; for he is lost, and for ever!' Then after a long pause she said, 'Is it Miss Trcherne?' and when the doctor said 'Yes,' she hid her face with her hands, but lay perfectly still. After some time she said, 'Don't be unhappy about the papers. If I had seen them it would have made no difference. He might perhaps have let me go back to him, but his heart would not have been with me. He has loved her for some time. You must tell him I'm bearing it well. I don't want him to be miserable on my account. I think, if you please, I should like to be alone a while.'

The nurse, a homely, ignorant woman, made the doctor a sign not to consent to this. Ghastly visions of what might happen if he did, flitted before her mind's eye; but the doctor knew better, and said, 'You shall be left alone; you are so good and brave that you deserve to have your way. Come, nurse.'

He went and saw some other patients, and an hour afterwards he looked in on Hester again. Her cheeks were wet with tears, but she was not actually crying; only from time to time tears of which she was all unconscious slowly welled into her eyes. He looked very anxious. He would have preferred a hearty outburst of grief. She tried to speak to him, but her voice failed her, and she could not utter one word. She held out a wan hand and looked gratefully in his face. He gave the nurse some directions in private, and bade her on no account leave Hester long alone. She lay very still after he was gone. Afternoon gave way to evening, and evening to night, and still she was lying there with wide-open eyes full of quiet misery. When the nurse spoke to her she answered, but it was easy to see that she preferred being left alone. 'Try to sleep,' said the nurse, in the early morning hours; 'a little bit of sleep would do you more good than anything. Shut your eyes, and then you will soon go over.'

Hester shut her eyes obediently, but they were soon wide open again.

'I had a sister who went wrong, too,' observed the nurse. 'Oh, miss, what she did suffer when he deserted her!'

Hester fixed eyes full of apprehension on the nurse's face. This was such plain speaking for a poor wounded girl to hear; but, alas! she could not complain of the view of her conduct which the woman was taking.

'He deserted her?' repeated Hester.

'Yes, miss; they all desert them sooner or later,' replied the woman.

A flood of tears rushed to Hester's eyes. The nurse's words had unsealed the fount of tears.

'Ay, cry, miss, do; it will do you more good than anything. It's terrible bad to bear, I know; but, miss, dear, I do hope what you are feeling now will drive you to lead a better life in future.'

'Oh, nurse, be silent! Do you want to kill me?' But that kind, though coarse-textured woman had said things which brought the truth to her mind. The whole current of her thoughts changed, and instead of lying there feeling herself a wronged and despitefully entreated woman, she began to wonder if she were but receiving her deserts.

CHAPTER XX.

PEDIGREE MAKING.

> Forbear a while,
> There's something tells me (but it is not love)
> I would not lose you.—*Merchant of Venice.*

'SHE does not love him, but she will accept his love if he offer it, and will go through life thinking little of the gift.' This had been Hester's bitterest thought after she had seen Daylesford and Josephine Treherne together. At that time, if Zeph had been asked if she would accept him she would have answered by a decided negative; a day or two later she would have denied the possibility of such a thing even with scorn; and now she was his engaged wife! How had this change been brought about? She knew of this other tie— she knew of a strong feeling in her own heart which ought for ever to have separated her from him. She was not a child to be talked into a marriage against her will, and besides that, who was there to try to persuade her? Not her dreamy preoccupied father, not her mother who so perfectly fulfilled the whole duty of woman according to Blake's conception of it, namely, that she should be an emanation of the man whom she had chosen. Zeph had not been surprised into the engagement. She had had time to think and carefully weigh the question ; but, alas ! when a man like Daylesford is weighed in the scales, so many other things, and most delightful and fascinating things, cannot fail to be weighed with him. Zeph's own life seemed to her to be dull, commonplace, and even tragic in the ugliness and meanness of its environment. She shuddered when she thought of it; her long visit to Berkhampstead had made her so alive to the horror of it that she could not bear the idea of returning home. It was so delicious to pass day after day knowing nothing of the weary struggle to make one pound do the work of two, and two servants do the work of three. Life in Lorne Gardens, as compared with life at the Castle, was like living down in a coal-pit instead of in the blessed light of day. And yet, after a while, she would have to return to that wretched existence. Her father could not stay at Berkhampstead for ever. All was beautiful and harmonious there, and it was so easy to be good. Sometimes she was a trifle dull, for she had not many resources of her own, but she had got into the habit of going into the library with her father, and he generally found her some little employment which made her feel busy. It was strange Daylesford did not come to see how they were going on ; sometimes she felt a little piqued at his indifference on that point, but if Mrs. Scatcherd said anything about it, she declared that she could not understand why he should leave London for such a quiet place. If he had come to the Castle there would surely have been a little more gaiety, and Zeph pined for gaiety, and most of all for another fancy ball. She had begun to forget about Hester, and the pain she had felt on first hearing of this *liaison*. These quiet weeks with her father and mother had done much to restore her calm, and yet in spite of tranquil days spent in peace and great delight at the pleasantness of the life she was then leading, Zeph could not quite forget. On the afternoon of July 27, Zeph was not doing anything particular, for Mr. Treherne needed little help just then; she was in the library, but only for the sake of companionship, and she was trying to make herself believe that she was enjoying a book she had in her hand. Suddenly she was called away, for Mrs. Scatcherd had come in the prettiest of pony-carriages to ask her to accompany her to a village about six miles off. ' It will do you good,' said she, kindly; ' you sit in the house too much; you mope! Not that moping seems to suit you badly—I never saw you look so pretty. Your complexion is lovely! I wish I were a pretty young girl like you, but I am quite old and plain.'

'Go into the drawing-room, and look at yourself in the glass, while I put on my things,' said Zeph, for Mrs. Scatcherd and she were standing by the hall-door; 'do go, and then I am quite sure you will see that you are not.'

'Oh, yes, I am; but I would not have come out in this dingy tussore if I had known what a radiant sylph was going to sit by my side. White does suit you, dear, you look quite delicious; and how clever of you to wear those becoming violet pansies. Put on that little straw hat of yours, and then I defy any one to resist you. You will be the queen of fairyland, and I shall be the nut-brown maid. It can't be helped. Be quick.'

Zeph was quick, and the pony made a brilliant little departure. The day was splendidly fine, but not too warm. The sky was cloudless, the air calm. Everything was steeped in sunshine. Zeph's heart bounded— she was happy, she knew not why. Perhaps it was the change of scene, for without quite knowing it, she was often dull. How could she be otherwise, living as she did with two old people whose sole aim in life was to identify themselves with the parchments they were always poring over. From the summit of a long low hill and far away on the road before them, Zeph and her companion saw a cab struggling slowly upwards. The sun glinted on the top of it and made shining white patches of light— the dust rose in clouds behind it.

'Oh, look at the dust that wretched cab is making!' exclaimed Mrs. Scatcherd. 'We shall be in the midst of it directly, and then good-bye to all our nice freshness of appearance! It is too bad—we make no dust.'

'But we must,' said Zeph. 'If it makes dust, we must make it too. We don't feel that which we make ourselves, perhaps.'

'I said I was old,' observed Mrs. Scatcherd, 'but there is one thing which used to torment me when I was a child that I remember as if it were yesterday, and I could not be more than three, if so much. I was so little that I just came up to the knees of the big people

who took hold of my hand whenever I walked
out ; and I used to be choked with the dust
they made. I can recollect the clouds of it
they made each step they took, and it just rose
to the level of my eyes and mouth. That is
one good of growing up—your breathing arrangements get to a better level. Do you
remember suffering from that?'

'I? Oh no,' replied Zeph, as if she were
disappointed at having been deprived of these
inconveniences; 'I have none of these memories—my youth was spent in a town.'

'I wish my age was!' said her companion,
fervently. 'I should like to know who is in
that cab—there is some luggage beside the
driver.'

'Some one for the Castle probably—perhaps a new servant.'

'Oh, no,' replied Mrs. Scatcherd, who was
intimately acquainted with the affairs of every
household within a radius of ten miles of her
own home. 'They are not changing any of
the servants at the Castle—I know that.'

' Perhaps it is Mr. Daylesford ? '

' Oh, you don't suppose that he would come in a cab—he would have telegraphed for the carriage. Fancy his coming in that thing ! '

' And he wrote to the butler about some arrangements yesterday—I know he did—he would not have done that if he had intended to come to-day.'

' He may have changed his mind—he must, for I do believe it is he ! ' exclaimed Mrs. Scatcherd, in great delight. ' But how sunburnt he is, poor dear, I should scarcely have known him ! ' She was right. It was Daylesford. He stopped the driver at once and got out of the cab to speak to them, looking very bright and handsome, but, as Mrs. Scatcherd had said, richly bronzed by Icarian sunshine. He expressed his delight at meeting them so unexpectedly. They did the same, together with warm congratulations on the happy termination of his anxiety. Mrs. Scatcherd, as usual, monopolised most of the conversation, but Zeph looked quietly pleased to see him.

When he had re-entered his cab, which now seemed dingier than ever, and they, too, had begun to pursue their way in an opposite direction, Mrs. Scatcherd said, 'My dear, I always thought that man was in love with you, but now I am absolutely convinced of it!'

Zeph made no reply, but when Mrs. Scatcherd looked to see why she was so silent, she saw that she was blushing violently. In truth, Zeph herself had seen something in his greeting which made Mrs. Scatcherd's words no surprise to her.

'You need not deny it. I am never deceived in things of that kind. That man is over head and ears in love with you, and you are a very lucky girl!'

Zeph, trembling with strong feeling, laid her hand on Mrs. Scatcherd's arm and said, 'I think you are forgetting what you yourself told me before Mr. Daylesford went away— about that—that girl, you know.'

At first Mrs. Scatcherd was puzzled by

Zeph's words, but when she added that last fragment of explanation, a light broke in upon her brain—she understood what she meant at once. 'It is he who is forgetting her, not I; and a very good thing too! Such disgraceful things must come to an end some time, and it ought to be a great comfort to you to know that you have helped to put an end to this. You have been the means of rescuing him from the clutches of this wicked woman—be thankful, my dear.'

'He ought to marry her,' said Zeph, in a low voice.

'Marry her! I should like to know who is going to do that!'

'I don't suppose you are right about his feeling for me,' said Zeph, completely ignoring what her friend had just said; 'but I am afraid I could never return his liking.'

'Not return his liking!' Mrs. Scatcherd stared at her in amazement. 'Not return his liking! I never heard anything so absurd in my life! Why, you might search the whole world through and not find any one so worthy to be loved! Any girl might be proud of him; he is a thoroughly fine fellow, manly and noble. Just think how splendidly he has behaved to his brother; and how rich he is, and handsome, and what a position he has!'

'Yes; but in spite of all that, a girl could not make herself love him if she were not inclined.'

'Oh, yes, she could. She would be a very foolish creature if she couldn't. Any girl of sense would contrive to love him somehow or other—that is, if she did not love some one else already'—added Mrs. Scatcherd unexpectedly, and at the same time she fixed a piercing look of inquiry on poor shrinking Zeph.

Zeph could not meet her gaze, her eyelids fell, and she said in a low voice, 'It is not any one I can ever marry.'

'Then if it is some one whom you can never marry, you ought to be wiser than go on thinking about him. My dear, you would be acting most madly if you refused Godfrey

Daylesford, supposing such a great piece of luck befell you, and he were to offer to you.'

'Mrs. Scatcherd, you forget what I cannot—you have no idea how that——'

'Stuff! Besides, it is your duty to save him. Nothing but really loving some good young girl can save him.'

'And very likely you are entirely mistaking his feeling for me.'

'Very likely,' replied Mrs. Scatcherd, with mock humility. 'I never was considered a person of much penetration! My dear,' she added with much fervour, 'I tell you again, that man loves you!'

'I wish you would not talk of it,' said Zeph, piteously. She herself was almost inclined to believe he did, but she could not bear to hear a half-formed thought put into words.

They spoke of other things; they made their call and set their faces homeward; they talked to each other, but in a dull subdued way, avoiding all mention of Daylesford. Zeph had a consciousness that she was each moment drawing nearer and nearer to a crisis in her life. Earnestly she wished that things had been rather different. There was that dark circumstance in Daylesford's previous history, and there was another and yet more potent obstacle. She still loved John Simonds. Do what she would, she could not forget him. Had it not been for these two obstacles, how brilliantly happy she might have been—that is, if what Mrs. Scatcherd had just said were true. Everything life could offer that was delightful would then have been hers. Daylesford was charming, and Daylesford was rich and great, and Zeph was ambitious to her heart's core.

'How you have been worrying yourself all the way home!' observed Mrs. Scatcherd when they reached the park gates. 'Your poor, dear face has shown me how you were tormenting yourself. And my dear child, your duty is so plain.'

'Oh, don't say any more about it,' pleaded

Zeph, looking weary with the distress of her own thoughts. They tried to keep up something that might be called conversation on other matters, as they drove through the long avenue; but it was a vain effort, and it was a relief when they came to the Castle. 'Good-bye, my dear,' whispered Mrs. Scatcherd. 'Take my words seriously to heart.'

Zeph went straight to her own room; she wanted to escape from sight, and had not much more time than was necessary to dress for dinner. Her manner was very subdued all the evening. She answered when she was spoken to, but did not originate anything. All that she could do was to look beautiful, and very gentle and sweet. Mr. and Mrs. Treherne stayed in the drawing-room all the evening as a compliment to their host. He could have dispensed with this act of self-sacrifice, for he had been hoping for a repetition of his former *tête-à-tête* with their daughter; but he was touched and pleased by Zeph's warm though unobtrusive sympathy when he told them how his brother had been saved. Mr. Treherne reported progress, too, and dwelt on some discoveries he had made, and there never was a chance of speaking to Zeph alone.

The next morning was not unlike the evening before so far as regarded restraint, but it was very wet. When breakfast was over, Zeph went to the window for a minute or two, and stood watching the heavy rain beating down the flowers outside and making great pools in the corners of the beds.

'Come, Zeph,' said Mr. Treherne; he had become accustomed to having her in the library with him.

'Oh, don't go to the library!' exclaimed Daylesford. 'Come and play battledore and shuttlecock in the corridor.'

'One of the battledores is broken,' answered Zeph, who was very much afraid of being left alone with him, for she had a presentiment of what was coming.

'Oh, but we will mend it,' said Daylesford; 'we will get your father to pick us out a nice strong bit of parchment from one of the charters in the muniment room.'

' My dear friend,' exclaimed Mr. Treherne, fervently, ' you are no doubt speaking in jest; but if you knew the fate of many a precious bit of parchment as well as I do, I think you would forbear. The second decade of Livy was used just as you want me to use your charter. One page only was rescued from an injured battle-dore. Think of that! one solitary page! Promise me—promise me solemnly—never to say such a thing again, even in jest.' Then he went away, and quietly, but decidedly and as if she preferred it, Zeph followed her father and mother.

Daylesford began to see that all the delicious opportunities of seeing her alone which he had once enjoyed were over. She now seemed to feel that her place was with her father and mother, and he was vexed to think that he had himself to blame for this; for it was he who, for the sake of showing Mrs. Treherne the castle and park, had suggested that Miss Tre·

herne should for once become her father's assistant. Zeph's manner was quite friendly, but he was certain that she wished to avoid him. He looked into the library once or twice —it did seem so strange to see her sitting there with the old folks—they seemed to take it as a matter of course that she should be by their side—pen in hand, making notes, copying something, or, more usually, doing nothing. Very soon he began to hate that room, and look upon it as a dismal pit expressly constructed to swallow up youth and beauty. He went there, for the third time, later in the day. She was looking tired; Mr. Treherne was lost in the depths of the inner room; Mrs. Treherne quietly knitting. ' The sun has come out, Miss Treherne,' said he; ' do give up work and take a little turn. If you think the garden too damp, we will go into the conservatories— there are some flowers I want you to see.'

She looked up in some distress, and put her finger on her lips. ' Don't say anything more about going out just now,' she whispered.

'Father wants me in a minute or two, I think.'
She whispered—did she not know that she
might have spoken in her usual voice—her
father had made up his mind to endure period-
ical visits from his kind host, and never to let
himself be disturbed by anything that occurred
when Daylesford was there?

'Mrs. Treherne will do anything he wants,'
pleaded Daylesford.

'Yes, but he likes me to be there in case
he has anything for me to do,' answered Zeph.

'Then let us go to the far bay-window
until he comes out of the muniment room.
You will be within reach of recall, and we can
talk without fear of disturbing him. Do come;
I want to tell you some of my adventures—we
have scarcely had a word together yet.'

Very reluctantly Zeph retreated with him
to the other end of the room. The window
was a wide bay, with a long low window-seat,
on which they found comfortable places side
by side. A writing-table stood in front of it,
and Zeph, who now seemed to think that she

could not exist happily without a pen in her hand, mechanically drew this table nearer to her and began scribbling on a sheet of paper. He gently took the pen from her and said : ' No ; you may have a pen in your hand when you are sitting at that other table, but while you are here, I mean to have your undivided attention.' She folded her hands in assumed meekness and sat dutifully looking at him.

He smiled and said, ' Are you taking me as part of your daily stage of duty ? ' He was so glad at having got her to himself, even so much as this, that he felt quite gay.

' I don't at all dislike duty,' replied Zeph. ' It grows on one.'

' It's a case of " seen too oft, familiar with its face," I suppose,' said he.

But Zeph's range of reading had not included the poem in question, and no ray of intelligence betraying familiarity with the quotation brightened her eyes. He did not mind that, he had not lost his heart to her because she knew where quotations came from. Just at this moment, Mr. Treherne emerged from the inner room and made his way to his own table with a bit of discoloured parchment in his hand. He was feasting his eyes on the sight of it as he went, and he carefully cleared a place to spread it out in safety.

'Now I must go,' said Zeph.

'Oh no, he has not so much as looked to see if you are there,' said Daylesford. 'Wait till he remembers your existence, at any rate.'

Zeph apparently resigned herself to this. Daylesford was anxious to take her beyond reach of a summons. He looked out of the window behind him and said, 'It is so fine outside now; that shower has made everything deliciously fresh. Do come out for a minute.'

'No, thank you,' said Zeph, rising; 'I ought to go back to my work;' and so saying she began to move.

'You surely would not be so unkind,' said he, venturing to lay a restraining hand gently on her arm. She dropped back into her seat in a moment to make him take his hand away.

'Your father is buried in that document,' said he, in a very low voice, for he was so afraid of reminding him of their presence; 'and you know you were not really doing anything.'

'You don't believe in my work!' she said, looking dissatisfied.

'Oh yes, I do; you must be quite a good antiquary by this time.'

'Quite. I know all about terriers now; and do you know, Mr. Daylesford, I can actually draw up a pedigree. I dare say you don't believe me, but I can.'

'Oh, can you? I very much want you to do something to my pedigree.'

'What is it?'

'To help me to make an entry in it.'

'I wonder whether I can,' she said.

'You certainly can.'

'How proud I shall be if I have learned enough to do it.'

'You can do it without knowing anything.'

'Ah, how you lessen the honour and glory!' she complained. 'I was so hoping for an opportunity of showing my newly acquired antiquarian knowledge.'

'But I shall give you an opportunity of showing me something I value a million times more than that,' said he, in a still lower voice. He looked so different from his usual self that she began to wish her father would call her back to his side, but he was hopelessly absorbed in the perusal of his parchment treasure. Again she looked at Daylesford, and saw his eyes fixed on hers with an expression so full of meaning, and meaning which she could not fail to understand, that she almost cowered beneath his gaze; and turning her eyes in another direction made things no better, for she still seemed to feel his fixed on hers, and knew what she should see in them if she dared to look round again. Blushing, trembling, and hardly able to speak from nervousness, she made a last great struggle to restore their interview to an easy footing, and pulled a sheet of paper towards her, saying,

'Let me show you how clever I am at

drawing up pedigrees—I will do yours, but I can't begin at the very beginning, for I don't know the names of all the people, and how things went in your family,—I mean if fathers always succeeded sons properly, or if collaterals sometimes came in.' She was in such a state of confusion and agitation, that she had no idea how she was reversing the usual laws of succession in this speech, and was only partly conscious how her voice was trembling. 'I shall have to begin with the husband of my dear benefactress, Phillis Arnold,' and as she named her, she involuntarily turned to look out on the lawn where her tombstone lay, a gleaming grey slab in a broad expanse of sunlit green.

Daylesford watched her as she wrote, and she wrote quietly for some time.

'You are doing it all right,' said he, 'so far as their names go; but you ought to give the dates of their births, deaths, and marriages, and you don't know them.'

'Oh, I shall easily get them from the

registers and tombstones in the church,' said Zeph lightly, for she was beginning to hope that she was going to escape the danger of which she had just been in such terror. She heard him say, 'Unhappily, you won't get all of them there.' Then she remembered the circumstances of his father's marriage, and what an unfeeling creature she must appear to him. 'Oh, how thoughtless I must seem to you!' said she, now looking sorrowfully in his face. 'Forgive me! My head is confused with other thoughts.'

'Mine is confused too, and yet it is only full of one thought,' he replied, 'and the sooner you know it——'

'Don't tell it to me now,' she exclaimed; she felt as if she would have liked to sink into the earth.

'Then I'll write it,' said he. 'Give me your pedigree, and I will add something which will make it entirely right according to my way of thinking;' and he took a pen and wrote something hurriedly. Then he laid a sheet of blotting-paper on it, and looked anxiously in her face.

'Father is getting so fidgety!' said Zeph; ' he hears us talking.'

'It can't be helped!' said Daylesford— never had Mr. Treherne's feelings been so disregarded before.

Daylesford folded the paper and gave it to her, looking fixedly at her as he did so. 'Read what I have written,' said he, 'and tell me if it is right.'

' Perhaps it is difficult to understand,' said she.

'No, not at all.'

' Difficult to answer then?'

' I hope not. Look at it—you are trying me too much. Read it, and remember that the happiness of my whole life is in your hands.'

' Don't ask me to read it while you are here,' said she, piteously.

He rose to go in a moment. Had he been alone with her he would have stayed to plead his cause, but as it was, with Mrs. Treherne looking up from her work every three or four minutes, and with the certainty that if he raised his voice Mr. Treherne would be disturbed and at once call Zeph back to her duties, he felt he could say nothing likely to move her. 'I'll go into the garden,' said he; ' you will make me unspeakably happy if you will come to me there.'

Zeph watched him leave the room, and then opened the folded paper. She saw the pedigree she had been trying to draw up, but at the end she saw some words in his handwriting.

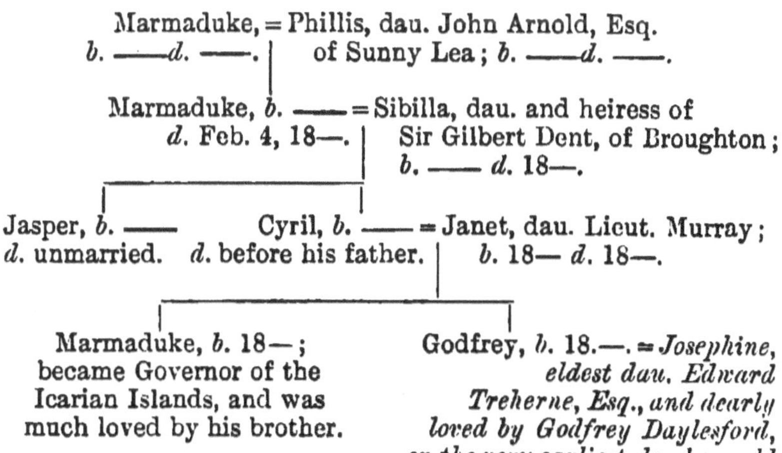

She sat in a kind of stupor—that which she greatly feared had come upon her. She saw him in the garden and could not but own that he was a man any woman might be proud of. He was handsome, kindly, and had generously offered her so much. And yet it was so difficult to know what to do! She sat buried in thought. Her head drooped lower and lower, and at last she laid it on the table and tried to still its throbbing.

Mrs. Treherne observed this and made her husband look.

'Zeph, my love,' said he, 'I hope you are not ill.'

'No, dear,' she replied, sitting up at once; 'not ill at all, thank you.'

'Come here, then, and let me have you near me,' said he.

She crossed the room with slow and faltering steps and sat down in her accustomed place —she even took up her pen.

'No, my child,' said he, 'you shall not do any more work for me to-day. You do not look well. You may give me that bit of writing you did after breakfast, I am ready for it now.'

Zeph, in a maze of confusion, began turning over the papers lying before her—her version of the Daylesford Pedigree, what she had copied, and other things. Seeing that she could not find what he wanted, he put out his hand to examine the papers himself. She took up the pedigree and gave it to him.

'Will you read that, father,' she said, 'and tell me what I am to do?'

'What is it?' he asked. 'What have you been doing?'

'What is it? A pedigree!' said Mrs. Treherne, who had come nearer and was reading over her husband's shoulder. Zeph rose and went to her father, put her arm round his neck, and laid her soft cheek against his.

'Dear father, help me,' said she. 'It is a fragment of pedigree that I drew up to show Mr. Daylesford that I had learnt something by sitting here with you, and he wrote that bit at the end, and that is how he says he wants his pedigree to be, father; and now he is in the garden waiting till I give him an answer.'

Mr. Treherne drew his head away from her that he might look in her face to see if she were in her sound mind. He had never thought of Zeph's marrying at all, much less of her marrying a man like Daylesford. His eyes were full of astonishment.

'Zeph, my child, are you in earnest? Mr. Daylesford has offered you his hand?'

'Yes, dear, he has, but——'

'Such a marriage exceeds my most sanguine hopes! My dear Zeph, a place in such a pedigree as the Daylesfords' is not offered to a girl like you once in twenty years!'

'But, father dear, I am in doubt whether I can love him enough to marry him.'

'Then you had better go to your room and take solemn thought with yourself. You must not accept him lightly. You yourself best know the state of your own feelings. Go, my dear, and take ample time to reflect.' Then, as this was a crisis in her life, and he loved her dearly, he added, 'My dear, would you like to have your mother with you? I will spare her to you, if you wish it.'

'No, thank you,' said Zeph; 'I had better be alone. Thank you for not trying to persuade me.'

She shut herself in her own room and tried to think she loved Daylesford, for a life linked with his would exactly suit her ambition. She could not deceive herself. She admired him, she liked to be with him, but he had never touched her heart, and she knew why. After more than an hour had passed, she resolved to write and say she could not marry him, and to give him the true reason, for she knew he would accept no other. She wrote her letter and sat for a long while looking at it. The sacrifice was too great for her, she could not send that letter. If she did she would lose a brilliant future—she would have to leave the Castle at once; she would never be invited there again; never be invited to anything by Godfrey Daylesford, but have to live in Lorne

Gardens just as she had lived before she knew him! She could not do it! Why should she sacrifice so much for the sake of a man she never intended to marry? She absolutely shuddered at the thought of Lorne Gardens. She tore up the letter she had written. It was a foolish letter she thought, but it had done her good to write it. She took a new piece of paper and wrote; 'It shall be as you wish some time,' put it in an envelope, and sent it to Daylesford. And thus was an engagement which brought such misery on others entered into.

CHAPTER XXI.

BECAUSE I HAVE SEEN HIM.

The bridegroom spoke low and led onward the bride,
And before the high altar they stood side by side,
The rite book is opened—the rite is begun,
They have knelt down together to rise up as one.
Lay of the Brown Rosary.

'AND now that the thing is done,' said Zeph, 'I do not intend to make myself miserable about what has gone before. I shall take all the good that comes in my way and enjoy it.' This she said to herself in the stillness of her chamber, but she had not the slightest conception of the amount of good (good according to her conception of the word) that would come her way. Before she was engaged to Daylesford she had been a pretty girl on a visit at the Castle, whose existence was to be made as pleasant as possible while she was there, but that was all. Now she was the great lady of the place, and every one treated her with a deference that at first made her uncomfortable. Daylesford himself was so happy and proud of her that every minute of her life seemed a triumph. Hitherto she had known nothing of such homage as this. She was almost distressed by it. And she was consulted about everything. She had suddenly become a person whose voice had weight in every discussion, and whose lightest wish was sure, if possible, to be gratified. She had the great happiness, too, of seeing that her father was delighted with her engagement. She taxed him with caring for it because it gave her the *entrée* of the Daylesford pedigree, but she knew that she did him an injustice and that he heartily liked her betrothed husband. Her days were now spent in a bewilderment of pleasures and arrangements. The 'County' came to congratulate—the county entertained them, and the most beautiful presents arrived daily. She had said that she would not allow herself to think of the past—it is scarcely too much to say that from the time when her engagement was made known she had no leisure to think of anything but each day's brimming measure of excitement and occupation. Long conversations with Daylesford and endless consultations with dress-makers and milliners, and letters to shops, and letters thanking people for wedding-presents, and hours spent in receiving pleasant visitors and paying pleasant visits made up the sum of Zeph's existence. Sometimes the thought flashed into her mind, ' I might have been sitting boring myself to death on my old black box in Lorne Gardens if I had not the sense to tear up that letter of refusal !' and she sighed a deep sigh of relief at having for ever escaped that woe. She was not even going back there to be married ! Mr. Treherne did not want to have to take a journey and leave his work for so long, and Zeph hated the thought of going; so she entreated Daylesford to let the wedding take place quietly in the little tumble-down

parish church close by.   Dr. Scatcherd was to
perform the ceremony, and Jemmy Benson,
the little boy who had been hiding in the
bedroom at the vicarage, on the eventful day
when Zeph had spent the morning there, and
who had become a great friend of hers, was to
help Jack to hold up her magnificent train.
Marrying quietly did not mean anything beyond the use of the word.   Zeph was to have
her due length of train and due richness of
silk, and she was to wear the diamonds that
her brother-in-law the governor had given her.
He was coming all the way from Santa Eulalia
to be present at the ceremony.   She was to
have four bridesmaids; but there was a little
vexation connected with the bridesmaids, for
she had had great difficulty in persuading her
sister Polly to be one of the number.   Polly
had refused, and the only reason she had given
was that she did not care about the engagement.   Polly had yielded, but her words had
left a sting, which on the very rare occasions
when Zeph had time to think of such things

still caused her pain. She could not help thinking sometimes of her own sisters and their sayings, but she never thought of the lover of her youth; and as for Hester, for the present, at all events, all remembrance of her was absolutely wiped out. If any one had told Zeph a week or two ago that a day would come when these things would pass from her mind, she would have laughed the idea to scorn—but such was the case now; her every thought was given to pretty dresses, jewels, carriages, court ceremonies, and all the rest was a tissue of bright hopes.

She was rather afraid of the governor. 'My dearest Zeph, you need not be afraid of him,' said Daylesford; 'he will love you, I am certain, both for your own sake and for mine.'

'I hope so, I am sure,' said she; 'you must promise me to tell him that both the Trehernes and Seatons are very good families.'

He was so much in love that he scarcely smiled, and when she went on to tell him that she was glad he had no other near relations,

he did not object to that either. The governor
came a fortnight before the wedding. He was
as handsome as his younger brother, and very
like him, but stronger, and perhaps cleverer-
looking, and he seemed to be at least ten years
older than Godfrey. His arrival doubled the
excitement; and now there was a constant
coming and going of London people and great
and small county neighbours. Miss Everilda
and Polly, Agnes and Jack were all at the
Castle now, and sometimes Zeph was in an
agony of apprehension lest Miss Everilda's
absurdities should disgrace the family, or Polly
or Agnes seem too infinitely below the Daylesford standard of propriety. Miss Everilda was
enraptured with the Castle—she sat for hours
together crouched on the stairs gazing at the
pictures, and jotting down any great thoughts
which occurred to her, in a crimson morocco
note-book. She wrote poems by the dozen,
and when writing of the two Daylesfords was
not above making use of Castor and Pollux.

Jack spent his time with the Scatcherd

boys, most of whom were Indian children and had no holidays. Polly and Agnes wandered about the house, garden, and grounds in perfectly new, well-chosen, and well-made dresses; for Miss Everilda would not have them lightly esteemed by their new great relations, and had supplied them with an outfit. They had blossomed out into fine handsome Teutonic goddess-like girls, and walked with their heads erect, and with honest clear eyes looked straight out on a world which was now treating their family with most unexpected kindness. They had never seen such a handsome place as the Castle. Zeph had paid visits to handsomer places with her betrothed, and knew that it was not by any means the most splendid nobleman's house in the kingdom, but they thought it was.

'It is such a pity that it is not really yours,' said Agnes, one morning when they were all in Zeph's room. 'Isn't it, Polly?'

Polly, who though much reassured as to Zeph's feelings, could not forget how John

Simonds had looked and spoken that day at the Kennedys, did not speak; she was often silent when the Daylesford honours and glories were under discussion.

'It is rather a pity,' said Zeph, pensively, 'especially as Marmaduke is always away; but then it is so nice to think of Godfrey behaving so well, and of the two brothers being such good brothers to each other.'

'They might have been just as good brothers,' replied Agnes, 'and the place have belonged to your Mr. Daylesford; as it is, it is lost! It can't be said to belong to either of them now.'

'Oh, it's all right!' exclaimed Zeph; 'they have arranged it as they think best, and I quite agree with them.'

'Well, I don't!' said Agnes, decidedly; 'and I think the governor puts himself too much forward, considering he has no right to anything but what his younger brother gives him.'

Zeph went away. She did not choose to

listen to this, and did not see what Agnes had to do with it. Zeph liked the governor, and the only fault that she saw in him was that he absorbed too much of Godfrey's time; but even that did not distress her much, for he was only to be in England that one fortnight. Zeph was on her way to the drawing-room to escape Agnes: on the stairs she encountered Miss Everilda.

'You are the luckiest girl in the world, my dear Zeph,' said she. 'You have a peerless lover and a princely brother-in-law, and you are young and beautiful, and have a career before you!'

There she touched a chord in Zeph's nature which vibrated at once. All this was not fulfilment—it was but the prelude to a long course of social triumphs. Godfrey and she were both fitted by nature to shine in the great world, and in the great world they would seek their happiness and find it.

'Mrs. Scatcherd is downstairs in the drawing-room,' added Miss Everilda, casually. 'I got so far as this on my way upstairs to ask you to go and see her, and then I had a good idea, and just sat down a moment to make a note of it.'

'Oh, I am so busy. She is always here!' said Zeph, impatiently.

That was true. Mrs. Scatcherd was persuaded that nothing could go right unless she herself lent a helping hand to it, and wanted every one to feel the same. Zeph had become rather intimate with her without much caring for her; principally because Mrs. Scatcherd was the kind of person who insisted on being intimate, and now Zeph bitterly regretted certain conversations which had taken place between them. She did not want to see her now, and went back to her room and asked one of her sisters to go and say politely that she was too busy to go downstairs.

'Too busy!' exclaimed Mrs. Scatcherd to Polly, who was the one who went; 'I can well believe it! What an exciting time this is! Even for me it is exciting, but then I really have had a great deal to do with bringing this match about. Just think what madness it would have been if she had refused him!'

Polly looked at Mrs. Scatcherd in amazement. The excited little lady was in full swing of exulting self-glorification, and wanted no answer to anything she said. 'Perfect madness! What queer miserable lives girls would often make for themselves, if they had not some one with judgment by their side! You will scarcely believe it, I know, but it took a great deal of persuading to make that dear sister of yours marry Mr. Daylesford. It must never go beyond ourselves, of course, but for a long time she was determined to refuse him! I need make no secret of all this with you —you know more about it than I do. You, of course, know why?'

Polly hesitated.

'And you know it is not as if she could have married this other man that she had such a fancy for,' added Mrs. Scatcherd. 'She never would have married him. Just fancy what folly it would have been to refuse such a first-rate marriage as this for a shadow! Well, let bygones be bygones—I shall always rejoice at the part I have been permitted to play. You must promise me not to mention this conversation—your dear sister might not like it. Promise me you won't, and let us say no more about it. I want to know if she has had any nice new presents.'

Polly sat for a long time after Mrs. Scatcherd's frivolous presence had at last been removed, doubting what she ought to do. It seemed so dreadful to speak to Zeph on such a subject as this—so wicked to leave her unspoken to. At last, slowly and thoughtfully, she walked upstairs to her sister's room. The two girls had of late appeared to have changed characters. Zeph was given over to dress and vanity, and Polly had become grave and anxious. She opened Zeph's door timidly. What she saw was this: Zeph, who, owing to her father's liberal salary and to his and Miss Everilda's boundless generosity on this great occasion, was in no want of money, had received a large box of hats from London on approbation, and was now standing at the looking-glass trying to get an idea of their effect. She was turning her head this way and that, and smiling her satisfaction at her own image in the glass.

Polly was very much afraid of speaking to Zeph about her marriage. Nothing but a strong feeling of anxiety and duty would have made her risk her almost inevitable indignation. She said, 'Zeph, I want to say a few words to you, dear.' Zeph knew in a moment that it was something that she would think disagreeable, and turned to face Polly in a way that made her so nervous that she uttered her thoughts in any words which presented themselves. 'Zeph, dear, do you never fear that you have chosen the wrong man?'

Polly's words fell so strangely on an intelligence which had separated itself from everything that did not concern the future, that for a moment Zeph did not seem to understand them. Then she coloured violently and said,

'Mary, how dare you? How can you say such a thing to me?'

'Because I have seen him!' said Polly, earnestly. 'I have seen him, and talked with him, and know how much he loves you, and how much right you have given him to believe that you returned his affection.'

Zeph turned away, but Polly saw that her face was crimson with the sudden shame of this.

'Mary, be silent!' she said. 'You know that I am going to be married in a few days. I wonder your own sense of decency does not prevent your speaking in such a way!'

Polly was by no means abashed, there was a great deal of honest fervour in her. She laid her hands on Zeph's shoulder, and said, ' Zeph, I am your own sister. I have loved you always, even when I seemed most disagreeable ; you know how we are situated ; you know that we have no father and mother to guide us. If I don't speak to you about this, no one will. I know I am not equal to you in any way, but be kind to me and listen. Do you love

Mr. Daylesford? Can you honestly say you do?'

Zeph tried to break loose from her sister's grasp, but that was no easy thing to do. Polly was strong in physical strength, strong in sense of right. Zeph ceased to contend with her. 'Answer, dear—answer truly,' persisted Polly.

'How stupid!' exclaimed Zeph, angrily; 'how ridiculously stupid you are! He asked me that, of course—Godfrey asked me that— and I said yes, and no one else has anything to do with it.'

'Then let me put my question in another way—Zeph, I will speak—you must listen!' For Zeph was saying 'No! No!' and trying to escape. 'Can you honestly say that you have ceased to love John?'

Zeph again flushed crimson, but this time with anger.

'Mary, this is unbearable!'

'No, dear, it is not. I entreat you to believe that I only speak because I love you.'

'Then if you speak because you love me,

sobbed Zeph, 'why do you speak of things likely to make me unhappy? All that is past and gone. I never think of it. I never want to think of it. I could not have been happy with John, he ought to have known it. Fancy a girl, brought up as I have been, being willing to begin another life of the same kind, but of her own making! The thing is absurd—if ever I thought of it I was a fool!—I should have died of a broken heart!'

Polly shook her head.

'You still have not answered my first question,' she urged. 'Do you love Mr. Daylesford?'

'Of course I do!' replied Zeph; 'am I not going to marry him in four or five days? If I said no, what would you do—take upon yourself to go and tell him that the marriage must he broken off?'

Polly sighed wearily, and said, 'Better even do that than let you marry him when you loved another man. Oh, Zeph! say what you will, I fear you do. Have some sense, have some true feeling, don't go madly into this just because all the outside trappings of the life Mr. Daylesford offers you are so pretty and handsome, and to your taste. Ask yourself if you love him enough to be a good, true wife to him whether he is rich or poor.'

'Of course I do, but I prefer to have him rich. Mary, I dare say, all this is well meant, but you are behaving very like a goose!'

Polly relaxed her hold. She told herself that she might have known that it was in vain for a poor blundering creature like herself to touch the heart or conscience of such a girl as her sister! She had tried and she had failed, and she knew it was in vain to say any more. Zeph meant to do it.   That was all.

'I have said my words of warning,' said Polly; 'you despise me for saying them. Give me a kiss to show that you are not angry with me. God grant you may never regret what you are doing!' and she left the room. These words rang in Zeph's ears. Her heart felt very full, and she sat for a long while without being able to move. She wished Polly had shown her the kindness of being silent on this subject. She had spent an hour or more much less pleasantly than any she had known for some weeks. Polly had stirred up certain thoughts, raised certain doubts. They were thoughts and doubts which Zeph was quite equal to laying to rest again, but not without an effort and assuredly not without pain.

When she went down to luncheon, however, her face was bright as usual. She showed no sign of consciousness or resentment in her treatment of Polly—no change in her behaviour to Daylesford. She could look in the face of both without an effort, and speak as light-heartedly as if nothing had happened; and five days afterwards, when she went to the village altar with him, and pledged her word to love, honour, and obey him, she did it unhesitatingly; she shed no tear, apparently harboured no doubt, shrank from no pledge.

CHAPTER XXII.

THE GOLDEN APPLE.

> Unbidden guests
> Are often welcomest when they are gone.—*Henry VI.*

> The Abominable, that uninvited came
> Into the fair Peleïan banquet-hall,
> And cast the golden fruit upon the board
> And bred this change ; that I might speak my mind
> And tell her to her face how much I hate
> Her presence.—*Œnone.*

SIX months had passed away and the Daylesfords were at home again after another long tour on the Continent. Godfrey Daylesford had enjoyed it much more than his wife had done, for he had been born and bred abroad and was more at home there than in England.

Zeph, who was not sufficiently well educated to take much pleasure in seeing far-famed places, and so imperfectly acquainted with foreign languages that she scarcely ventured to open her lips, especially in her husband's presence, would gladly have returned to her own country before winter. To her London was everything. She had always been aware of the joys it held in its keeping for those who were properly equipped to enter into them, and now she, thanks to her own youth and beauty, and to Daylesford's position, was, as she fondly hoped, so equipped, and she ardently longed for a full measure of them. It was April when she and her husband reached England once more. They had travelled quickly at the last, and Zeph was so tired that it had seemed desirable to stay the night at Dover, but her impatience to get to her journey's end was so great that they left by an early train next morning.

'Oh, I am glad we are back!' said she, turning from the bright landscape she had been enjoying from the railway-carriage windows to her husband. 'How lovely everything looks!' He smiled affectionately; it was so natural that after being so long a wayfarer she should pine to be at rest in her own home; but England had never yet been a home to him.

'Here we are!' said he, two hours later, and Zeph with some emotion looked at the house which she was now going to enter as mistress, and remembered that evening more than a year ago when she and Jack had been so amazed with the splendour they had seen by stolen glances from the outside. She was so engrossed by the thought of this, that she did not observe that Daylesford was waiting to help her out of the carriage.

'Come, dear,' said he, taking her hand; 'won't you come?'

She walked into the house with conscious pride.

'Welcome home, my darling,' said he.

She put her hand in his and felt that he was very kind and good to her. He looked round, but saw no familiar face, for there was an entirely new staff of servants; he had thought it better that his old life and his new

should be kept altogether apart. The other
servants had known Hester, and some of them
had shown a regard and pity for her far above
the wont of their kind; but they were gone,
and she was gone, and he was now walking
across the hall with a new love who was his
wedded wife. And yet, though he was pas-
sionately attached to Zeph, and felt her soft
little hand lying in his, he could not repress a
host of memories, and at every turn he seemed
to see a ghostly image of poor ill-treated, for-
saken Hester. He sighed heavily and felt the
trouble of this gathering about him, but he
made a violent effort and turned to look at
Zeph. She was gazing around on every side,
and all seemed very magnificent to her. They
went into the breakfast-room which looked
into a large garden, and then they were left
alone.

'Godfrey,' she said very gently, 'I feel
such a poor humble little creature now that
you have brought me here. I don't think I
am good enough for you.' She had not ex-

pected to feel this, and was surprised to find herself doing so.

'My darling,' said he, kissing her, 'you are a thousand times too good for me!'

Zeph was easily persuaded that this was the case, and then he began to wonder what they had better do to spend the time till luncheon was ready, which it would not be for half an hour. Zeph was guided to her own room, where she took off her outdoor apparel, and then looked curiously at some closed doors near. She was longing to see the house, but she thought that the proposal to go over it ought to come from him, and it was one that he was never likely to make, for he did not think there was anything worth showing. She returned to the breakfast-room, and somewhat discontentedly strolled to one of the windows and looked out to see if there was a pretty view from it, and then she sank into a chair and was soon half-buried in thought, half-occupied in gazing at all she saw from the open window. The day was fine, but vexed

by a never-ending contention between sun and
wind. The sun set its mark on the glistening
upturned leaves of evergreens which had borne
the burden and cold of the winter; the wind
dashed the leaves about until they almost
dazzled her as they flashed backwards and
forwards. The flower-beds were filled with
daffodils which tossed their heads in the breeze,
but did not remind her of Wordsworth's poem,
for she had never happened to read it; but
there was an exquisite almond tree, and the
tender pink petals rained down, and the sweet
scent of the rosy blossoms filled her soul with
delight. She was by the open window; he
was standing by the fire, for he had found a
table on which a large heap of letters was
lying, and from these he was culling one or
two which seemed to promise to be interesting.
What quantities of letters there were, and what
piles of prospectuses of new companies! How
easy it seemed to secure ten or twenty per
cent., and what foolish self-restraint not to
accept the offer of it! Daylesford rarely

opened one of these, but he gradually became more interested in examining his letters, and the noise he made in converting some of them into roughly-executed balls which he flung angrily into the grate roused Zeph from her dreamy state of wonder at the strangeness of having exchanged Lorne Gardens for Ambassadors' Gate, and fear lest by any chance this new life which lay before her looking so full of promise might after all fail to fulfil her expectations.

'My dear Godfrey,' she exclaimed, 'what a noise you are making with those papers! I wish I had as many letters as you have.'

'Letters, dear? Bills, some of them paid long ago; begging letters, circulars, all kinds of things one never reads more than a word of. You need not wish for such letters as these. Besides, you have a little pile of your own there on the mantelpiece. Why don't you open them?'

'What an unfeeling husband you are not to have told me that before! Do you suppose

that I should have sat all this time looking out
of the window, if I had known that there were
any letters for me?'   And she took possession
of a tolerably large packet, which when the
circulars and invitations to inspect milliners'
show-rooms and other useless communications
of the like kind were weeded forth, still yielded
a few letters.   She gazed at the address with
pleasure, though Godfrey always told her she
had no legal right to be called the Honourable
Mrs. Daylesford.   One letter was from Polly,
from Seaton Court, where she was paying a
visit to Miss Everilda which had already lasted
six weeks.   Zeph could not but remember that
Alnminster was within a drive of Seaton Court.
But Polly was not the kind of girl to mention
John Simonds—Zeph had no fear of that.
Polly had nerved herself to make that one last
appeal just before the marriage, and having
failed then, would now for ever hold her peace.
She was well and happy.   Miss Everilda was
very kind to her.   There was little enough in
Polly's letter beyond a welcome home, but

Zeph thought that she detected a certain restraint in her style which betokened much suppression. 'She is seeing a good deal of John, I suppose,' thought Zeph, 'and she has difficulty in avoiding all mention of him.' She put the letter down with a certain dissatisfaction. Polly's style chilled her.

There was nothing to chill her in the next letter which she opened. It was from Mrs. Scatcherd. That lady, now as ever, seemed determined to take for granted that she was Zeph's dearest friend—the artificer of her high fortune, the buttress of her life. 'I have heard with the greatest joy from the dear old people at the Castle;' Zeph gasped—how dared she speak thus of her father and mother?—'that you are coming home on April 3. Of course I shall come to you, my dearest, as soon as possible. If you feel as I do, every hour will seem a week until we meet. I don't think I can wait until you write to invite me. I will hurry up to town to see you on the 4th. I should like to go on the 3rd, but must give you time to recover the fatigue of your journey. This will enable me to bring you the last news of your dear father and mother. Mrs. Treherne says that she is going to write to you herself by this post, but I imagine that she is almost certain to find something come in her way at the last, so it is a good thing I have decided to come, for I shall be able to supply you with the last news of them. Do not imagine that it is inconvenient to me to leave home ; of course I would do it even if it were, but the doctor says he will spare me for a week or so. I think you will want me at least a week, and shall therefore come prepared. I am more than glad to accept his kind offer to spare me, for the boys are having their Easter holidays, and you can guess what that means. As he has no teaching just now, he must struggle with them as best he can in the absence of his assistant, who is away too, and I cannot help thinking that this, though disagreeable, will be such a complete change of work that it will do him good. I hope and trust some of it will be physical, for if ever two boys stood in need of a good caning the two Lawrences do, and your friend Jemmy Benson is about as bad. I shall be perfectly delighted to see you again, dear, and I hope and trust you will be equally pleased to see me.'

'My dear Godfrey!' exclaimed Zeph, putting this letter in his hand, 'Mrs. Scatcherd says she is coming to stay with us, and that she will be here to-morrow.'

Zeph scarcely knew whether she wanted to see her or not, but her husband had no doubt on the subject. 'Did you ever ask her to come?' he inquired.

'I, Godfrey, when I had only just been invited to stay in the house myself?' she replied.

'Then she is a most impudent woman! We won't have her here. She wants to get away from the boys and to buy her spring dresses, but you don't wish to see her for so long, Zeph. You can't; it's impossible!'

'I don't want to see her for a whole week,

and when we have just come home too. She
is kind, but she forces her friendship too much
on us. But she is coming—we cannot stop
her.'

'Oh yes, we can. Write and say that we
shall see her in her own home, that we are
going to Berkhampstead to-morrow to see your
father and mother. I'll telegraph—that will
be better.'

'But are we really going?'

'Yes.'

Zeph was half regretful. She dearly loved
her father and mother, but she wanted to stay
at home. She had not spent twenty-four hours
in the same place for nearly three weeks.

'I wish I could see Agnes,' said she; 'she
and Jack are at home. If the Scatcherd boys
are having their holidays, Jack is having holidays too. I wonder they don't come to see
us.'

Daylesford rang the bell. 'Send the carriage to 5 Lorne Gardens, De Manvers Town,
for Miss Agnes Treherne and her brother. Say

that your mistress has come home and wants to see her.'

'I'll send a line,' said Zeph, though in her heart she rather admired this regal way of doing things. 'Our change of plan has put her out; no doubt she came last evening.'

'She did, ma'am,' said the man, 'and a young gentleman came with her.'

Zeph scribbled her note and then opened a bulky epistle from Miss Everilda, but on further inspection she found that a great part of it was a poem.

'Hail, beauteous bride of seven sweet moons,' read Zeph.

'Is there nothing about the bridegroom?' asked Daylesford. 'How bridegrooms do get left out!'

'It's all about the bride,' said Zeph, 'and I almost think I shall read it some other time.' Daylesford laughed. 'There is a letter from her, I will read that,' said she.

'It will be just as high-flown,' he remarked.

It was. 'Sweet child,' wrote Miss Everilda,

' when your eyes fall on this you will be in your husband's ancestral home.'

' We have a seven, fourteen, and twenty-one years' lease,' said Daylesford, ' and nearly eighteen months of it are gone !　Go on.'

' You are basking in the purple splendour of his star-like love.'

' Let us have that again.　You might alter the arrangement of those words just as you pleased without making any difference to their want of sense.　I don't think I ever——'

' Mrs. Scatcherd,' said the footman, suddenly opening the door to allow that lady to enter.　She came precipitately forward, threw her arms round Zeph and embraced her tenderly. Then she put her half a yard away from her to feast her eyes on the sight of Zeph's beloved face, and then fell to kissing her again, doing it deliberately and pecking at favourite spots on her cheeks just as a bird pecks at the rosiest and ripest part of a cherry.　Daylesford meanwhile stood watching this ceremony with every mark of impatience, to the great discomfiture of Zeph, who occasionally saw his face over Mrs. Scatcherd's shoulder.

At last Zeph succeeded in breaking away from this effusive greeting. 'I have this moment read your letter,' said she. 'We thought that to-morrow was the day on which you proposed to come to town.'

'No, not to-morrow; to-day, the day after your arrival. I should have liked to have been here to welcome you, but I know husbands like to be alone on such occasions to show their wives their new home, and all that kind of thing.'

'We have only been in the house about three quarters of an hour,' said Daylesford, very coldly.

'We slept at Dover; I was so tired,' added Zeph, almost apologetically, 'and I have not seen the house yet.'

'Then do let us go and explore it together, said Mrs. Scatcherd, nothing daunted. 'I dare say Mr. Daylesford will be glad enough to let us find our way about alone.'

The way Mr. Daylesford was most anxious that she should find was that which would take her most quickly to her own home again. He had never much liked this woman, and latterly, when he had seen more of her, he had actually disliked her. He had observed how she forced her acquaintance on Zeph, and intended to put a stop to this persecution. But how to do it? Mrs. Scatcherd was the kind of person who, if thrown out of a house by the door, would re-enter it by the window. No doubt in the end she would have to be got rid of as such persons often are. Daylesford would be compelled to exert all his influence to secure good preferment for her husband.

'Do let us go and explore the house if you have not seen it; but I thought you had— I thought you came here before you went abroad,' said Mrs. Scatcherd.

'No; we did intend to do so, but we went abroad at once.'

'We must not go over it yet,' said Zeph.

' My youngest sister is coming directly ; let us wait for her.'

' But there are so many things I want to say to you alone,' pleaded Mrs. Scatcherd. ' However, as I am going to spend a week here I shall have plenty of time to talk. Besides, here is luncheon.'

' I regret to say that we are going to Berkhampstead to-morrow,' observed Daylesford ; ' my wife naturally wants to see her father and mother.'

Mrs. Scatcherd looked dismayed. ' To-morrow ! But that is such a very short time. Couldn't you put it off a little longer ? ' Zeph looked at Daylesford.

He shook his head. ' It would be very heartless not to let them have a look at their daughter after she has been away so long.'

' Oh, they are perfectly happy with their work among the old papers. You know their ways well enough by this time to be sure of that. When once they are in that library, I don't suppose they ever remember that they have a daughter.'

That same thought had often occurred to Daylesford, but now he wanted to make use of their parental feelings to escape from a visit that was wholly unwelcome to him.

'They really don't care to have any one with them,' continued Mrs. Scatcherd, eagerly. 'I made my way into the library where they were at work once or twice, just to see if I could cheer them a little, and I am almost certain that they wished me away.'

If Mrs. Scatcherd could entertain any doubt about Mr. Treherne wishing her away when she had the hardihood to invade his very sanctum, of what avail would any resistance be to her intended visit to Ambassadors' Gate? Daylesford was silently considering how best to meet this difficulty. She turned to Zeph and said, ' Go to Berkhampstead next week. Let us drive there together. I have often thought I should like to drive home from London for once. It must be very pleasant ; do let us do it this time. I have not taken a return ticket.'

' Oh no,' said Daylesfcrd, imperatively ; ' we must go to-morrow. We shall be happy to give you a bed for to-night.'

This was not what Mrs. Scatcherd intended, but the arrival of Agnes and Jack put an end to the discussion for a while. After luncheon Mrs. Scatcherd insisted on going over the house with Zeph and Agnes. Jack professed to follow them, but was soon absorbed by a book in the library.

' Dining-room, breakfast-room, library, and billiard-room, downstairs,' enumerated Mrs. Scatcherd. ' It's an awfully large house for London. Do you know the rent ? '

' Oh no,' said Zeph, who was almost shocked at the question.

' What a quantity of books there are in the library,' said Mrs. Scatcherd. ' I often wonder what people want with books. By the time I have run through the daily paper and two society weeklies I know all I care for.'

Upstairs there was a large drawing-room and the bedroom Zeph had already seen, and there was a very pretty sitting-room at the back communicating with a bedroom and dressing-room. The drawing-room met with their highest approval. It was full of lovely things of all kinds, but when they saw the suite of rooms behind, all three ladies exclaimed, ' What charming rooms ! '

' So homelike ! ' said Zeph.

' So elegant ! ' added Mrs. Scatcherd.

' So beautifully furnished ! ' murmured Agnes. ' There is everything that any one can possibly want.'

That was true; there was a piano, there were books—two lovely white bookcases quite full of them—and there were water-colour drawings on the wall which were a delight to behold. Comfortable chairs and sofas were placed in inviting corners, and on every table were the most exquisite flowers all breathing of the country and of Berkhampstead. Zeph's heart filled with rapturous delight. She had never so much as imagined such a perfect room. She knew that Godfrey had done all that was needed to make his house pretty to receive her, and this was the result. The mark of his generous heart and fine taste was set on all before her. This was to be her own room; here she would sit daily. All was his gift to her, and it was very good and beautiful. And those books; she knew how deficient her education was, but she would read every one of them for his sake. 'I shall always sit here,' she exclaimed enthusiastically. 'I shall never wish to be anywhere else! It is the prettiest room I have ever seen.'

'And how nice it is to have the bedroom opening out of it,' said Mrs. Scatcherd. 'We have not seen that yet. It's just as pretty as the sitting-room, and that is all there is on this floor except the dressing-room.'

'These rooms are far prettier than those I am to have,' said Zeph. 'I like them much better.'

'They are beautiful!' exclaimed Agnes, in

great delight. ' Zeph, you have done well to marry Mr. Daylesford.'

They visited each room in turn.

' Those three rooms form the prettiest suite I have ever seen,' said Mrs. Scatcherd, who had up to this time been making her observations in silence. ' They are quite shut off from the rest of the house, they are charming. So much taste has been shown in choosing the furniture.'

' It is exquisitely chosen,' said Zeph ; ' look, Agnes.' But Agnes was not there; she had strayed away into the drawing-room, and was wondering whether fate might perhaps have a Mr. Daylesford in store for her.

' I shall be so grateful to Godfrey,' said Zeph, warmly ; ' I shall thank him so much. I ought to do it, and I will.'

' Well, my dear, I am not quite sure that if I were you I would say much about it,' replied Mrs. Scatcherd, who never could allow anything to be done without giving her opinion. ' I am not sure it is advisable.'

' Of course it is advisable,' said Zeph, impetuously; ' it would be most ungrateful not. What can you mean ? '

' Well, my dear, I may as well tell you that I think it is not at all impossible that this pretty suite may have been furnished for some one else. A woman's taste has been consulted, I am sure; perhaps it was furnished for that—that other person.'

Zeph, whose heart had a moment before been all aglow with affectionate thankfulness to Daylesford for his love and kindness to her, started back at these words as if she had been stung. A painful blush mounted to her cheeks, the very tips of her ears were scorched with its strength.

' Be silent ! ' she exclaimed angrily; ' how dare you say this to me? If you have no sense of what is due to yourself, I will not allow you to forget what is due to my husband, and even to me.'

' Why, my dear Mrs. Daylesford——' said

Mrs. Scatcherd, turning to the angry girl with an air of wonder.

Zeph flung off the hand Mrs. Scatcherd had dared to lay on her arm, and said, ‘ Don’t speak to me !　I won’t listen to a word you say.’

‘ Oh, but you ought not to——’ she began once more.　But Zeph covered her ears with her hands and looked at Mrs. Scatcherd with eyes which did not fail to express even to such an insensitive person as she was, some of the anger her words had aroused.

‘ Oh, I beg your pardon, I am so sorry, I am indeed !　I had no idea——’ she stammered vaguely.

‘ You can’t have one womanly——’ began Zeph, but at this moment Agnes returned, and both were obliged to be silent.

‘ You may go over the rest of the house with Mrs. Scatcherd, if you like, Agnes,’ said Zeph ; ‘ I am not going.’

Mrs. Scatcherd was about to speak, but Zeph motioned her to the door, and some undefined feeling constrained the wretched little creature to obey Zeph's indignant gesture.

Mrs. Scatcherd had great faith in time, and little knowledge of heart wounds for lack of material on which to make experiments. 'Give her a little time to be alone,' thought she, 'and she will forget all about it.' So she went on her progress through the rooms with Agnes, who knew Zeph's way so well that she was certain something was very much amiss, but could not imagine what it could be. No sooner were they outside than Zeph shut and bolted the door against them, and then she struggled to a seat and burst into passionate tears. How her fine fabric of happiness had crumbled away beneath this woman's coarse touch! Just a minute before Zeph had been so happy, so grateful, so sure of Godfrey's love and goodness, and this wretched creature had come and with one word had destroyed all her pleasure in life. All her joy in her home was gone; all her happiness with Godfrey was over. It was hateful to be reminded of that wicked woman of other days. Zeph had known about her before, but somehow or other she had all but forgotten her existence. Now Mrs. Scatcherd had made it impossible for her to live an hour in that house without thinking of its former occupant. This room which was to have been her own favourite abiding place was now a very well-spring of poisoned thoughts. All she saw had been devised for that other person—everything that was pretty had been bought for her—here she had lived and moved, and here memories of her must for ever linger. Zeph could not control her tears—her cheeks were blistered by them.

Agnes came to the door and knocked.

'Let me in, dear,' she pleaded; 'I am alone, and I want so to be with you.'

'I cannot. I am resting. I am not ill, but I am very tired,' said she, doing violence to her grief and speaking calmly. 'Go away now, dear, and talk to Godfrey. Don't tell him that I say I am tired. I am coming down very soon.'

Agnes went, but she did not obey her sister. She told Daylesford that she was sure Zeph was either so tired as to be ill, or very much distressed about something, and he stole away to comfort her. Zeph was not familiar with the house and did not know that there was another way into that suite of rooms besides the door now under her control.

'My darling,' he said, full of concern, ' you ought to have stayed another day at Dover. I was sure we ought at the time.'

Zeph recognised in a moment that it was her duty to bear what she was now suffering alone. She had known about this when she married; how was it that she had not taken into account all that it might lead to? Daylesford had seated himself on the sofa by her side, his arm was round her now. She had half turned away from him; he was not quite the same to her as he had been before, but it was impossible not to feel his kindness.

'Forgive me, Godfrey,' said she, ' I am

foolish—strange thoughts have been coming into my mind.'

'Forgive you, dear,' he said, so kindly that Zeph began to weep again.

'What thoughts, Zeph?' he said. 'Tell your own husband.'

'I cannot,' said she. 'Don't ask.'

'Ah, how tired you are!' said he. 'Lie down on the sofa and rest, and perhaps you may sleep.' He could not believe that she was really suffering from anything but fatigue, and brought some rugs and covered her warmly, and then he stooped and kissed her. 'I am going to leave you alone,' said he. 'It is the truest kindness.'

'Yes,' she replied, for she longed for solitude.

'Is there anything I can do for you?' he asked, still unwilling to leave her.

'Send Mrs. Scatcherd away!' she said.

He almost wondered at her vehemence, but he went downstairs to try to do it. How little did he know the lady he had to deal with! She was in the drawing-room, and when he entered she said, 'I have been thinking a little about plans, Mr. Daylesford ; you say that you are both going to the Castle to-morrow?'

' Yes,' he said doubtfully, fearing an unforeseen trap.

' Then, as I came prepared to stay a week, and have my husband's leave to do so, and so seldom go away, couldn't I just stay on here and do all the little things I want to do, even if you do go to Berkhampstead ?'

He was half inclined to smile, for this was such a very odd arrangement for a person to make who had, according to her own statement, come to London solely because she could not be absent from Zeph. Now she was ready to let Zeph go to Berkhampstead, and herself stay behind.

' Yes, of course you can,' said he, ' if you like to do it.'

This last clause was added solely for his own amusement. She took no notice of it. She had gained her point, and contented herself with saying 'Thank you.' Zeph said thank you, too, when her husband told her about it just before dinner. She rose from her sofa wearily. She must go downstairs and appear to be on good terms with Mrs. Scatcherd; Godfrey must never know what had occurred.

CHAPTER XXIII.

THE FLUSH OF THE ALMOND BLOOM.

> ‘ Fool, sayde my muse to me, look in thy heart and write.’
>
> Sir P. Sidney.

ABOUT seven miles from Alnminster, on the great North Road, was Seaton Court, and here Miss Everilda lived in lonely state. Every one’s life is said to consist of a series of compromises, but hers involved more than fell to the lot of most people, and she was unfitted by nature to carry them out successfully. Her father, Adam Seaton, had been an ordinary hunting, shooting, hard-riding, hard-living country squire and magistrate, with a very kind heart and a rather weak head. He always followed his inclinations, but fortunately his inclinations never led him to do much harm to any one but himself. He was what the people around him called 'a fine, free-spoken, open-handed gentleman, who would not let a body come to grief for want of a pound or two to set him up on his legs again.' Many a pound he gave away, and all day long there was a constant stream of people coming to the back door to say that the squire had sent them to get a bit of dinner, or a glass of ale, or a basketful of garden stuff. Miss Everilda loved her father dearly, though no day ever passed without his inflicting a deadly wound on her tender susceptibilities. Tobacco-smoke and the smell of whisky and water were not an atmosphere for the delicate plant of poetry to thrive in, and yet that atmosphere hung about Seaton Court all day long. The house too was overrun with great rough dogs which often all but knocked her down, so indiscriminating was their attachment. Mrs. Seaton was a quietly kind woman who set herself to help the poor in a very different way. She admired her husband's pity for them, but did not approve of the form it took. She often told him that none of his dependents would ever do any good so long as they knew that they had only to come to him and at once find themselves lifted out of all their difficulties by his liberality. She tried to make them help themselves—she set on foot clothing-clubs and schools and things of that kind, but the triumph of her life was the establishment of a savings bank of which she was sole manager and clerk. The cottagers entrusted her with their little savings and she promised them a clear five per cent. interest; and so great was her business ability, that she was able to keep her word without loss to herself, and so profound their confidence in her that this undertaking grew larger and larger, until the fame of it spread over all the country side, so that when the good lady died a year or two after her husband, it was comparatively speaking quite a large con-cern. And now came a great difficulty for Miss Everilda. She had tenderly loved both parents, and would not for any consideration allow her mother's good work to perish because of her own neglect, and yet she had neither her mother's love of it nor her talent for management. Miss Everilda, who would have liked to inhabit an ideal world in which every one would roam over sunny plains or sit in shady gardens or groves, clad in flowing white garments composed of the simplest materials—say for instance a large fine white linen sheet arranged with the soul-sufficing grace and perfection of the drapery of a beautiful Greek statue—suddenly found herself obliged to descend to details of the most sordid nature, respecting calicoes which men called unbleached, and woollen fabrics of a coarseness altogether beyond the range of her experience. She had to fill her mind with knowledge of subjects for which she had no liking—she had to carry on the work of a savings bank and give five per cent. interest on all deposits when she was almost incapable of doing a sum in simple addition. She strained every nerve to do these things well because she respected her mother's memory too much to abandon her undertakings, but it is needless to say that she managed everything so ill that it cost her a hundred times more trouble than it had cost Mrs. Seaton, and as she had no fixed hours for doing work of this kind, she never had five minutes she could call her own. She scraped through her difficulties somehow, but she could not have done so if she had been a poor woman.

Her filial piety was not shown to her mother alone. All the dogs which had been such a nuisance to her in the days of their youth and beauty were still allowed to feel themselves at home in the sitting-rooms at Seaton Court, even though they were beginning to be blear-eyed and unsightly with age. 'My father would have liked it,' said Miss Everilda, and that was enough for her. Her young cousin Polly's presence was a great boon to her. She did not believe that she could ever let Polly go back to London again. Polly kept the savings bank account, Polly could 'do things in fractions,' though what advantage that might represent to Everilda Seaton was doubtful, for she was not the person to make any payment in fractions.

Polly could teach in the school, could send back a woman's banking-book without sending her a long poem by mistake, and altogether was a most useful person to her cousin.   Then Polly drew her forth from her 'study,' and led her away into the green fields and pleasant lanes, or they drove into Alnminster to hear the glorious cathedral service, and thus the wholesome element of change was introduced into her life.

'And to think of my having lived so many years without knowing you, my dear,' said Miss Everilda one morning.   'I might have had you here years ago if I had but known you would come.   Your poor dear mother offended all the Seatons by the way she neglected them after her marriage.   It was just as if she had shaken them off and never wished to see any of them again.'

'She is such a good wife to father.   She sacrifices everything and every one to him.'

'Yes, it is beautiful—most beautiful!' repeated Miss Everilda, meditatively, 'but if all marriages were like hers, people would think more than twice before they gave up their freedom. I should not like any of you dear girls to marry and have to live in that way.'

'We should not like it either,' exclaimed Polly. 'None of us could do it.'

'I suppose not. At all events Zeph has married very differently.'

'Indeed she has. Zeph would never have been happy with a poor man.'

Miss Everilda sighed and said, 'If she had been very much in love with any poor man, she would have married him.'

'Mr. John Simonds,' said a servant, appearing most unexpectedly, and John Simonds followed him into the room. He had got into the way of walking over from Alminster sometimes on his half-holidays to see the two ladies, and his visits were a pleasure to both of them. Sometimes he stayed for dinner, and Miss Everilda sent him home in her carriage. Polly was so startled by his appearance just as her cousin was saying something which had such a personal application to himself, that she could not help blushing, but no one saw her blush but Miss Everilda, who instantly suspected a love affair, and invoked a benediction on their young affection. Scarcely had she exchanged greetings with the newcomer before she saw in her mind's eye a sheet of fair white paper, with the first lines of a poem, in which she likened young love to the tender flush of the almond bloom. What was to rhyme to bloom ? Tomb was not the right word, and yet it would keep thrusting itself forward. She liked ' flush of the almond bloom ' and was resolved to find a good rhyme to it. Boom, loom. Time's loom and the web of their sweet fortunes might be worked in, but she must first see if she could not get something better. Gloom, doom. All the words seemed very ominous and unpropitious. She was proceeding to further researches when she suddenly found that while her mind had been given to this, Mr. Simonds had been talking to her, and that Polly had answered one speech for her and was now answering another. Then she heard her ask a question, to which the neglected guest replied :—

'No, I am afraid that there is no chance of a reprieve, and I don't think he will try to save himself by accusing the two others.'

The Assizes were going on in Alnminster, and there was a very heavy calendar. During the last two days a murder case had occupied much attention. There was not much evidence, for the crime had been committed in a lonely house in the country. The accused had solemnly protested his innocence. The facts of the case had however been very much against him, fatally so indeed, unless he could bring home the guilt to some other person; this he had made no endeavour to do, and he had been condemned to death. Public feeling was much stirred, for a very large section believed that he could have done this with complete success, but had refrained, for the persons whom he would have had to accuse were his own wife and her brother. The prisoner bore a good character ; the wife's character seemed to be less good, and her brother's was so bad that he could get no work at home and was about to emigrate.   The brother and sister had avowedly been on the spot a great part of the time, and had even taken part in the beginning of the struggle with much enjoyment, but they said that they had retired from it at a certain point, and they left it to be inferred that the prisoner had not done so until he had committed the crime.   The evidence of a passer-by had seemed to corroborate this, and yet a very considerable portion of the public refused to believe it, and regarded the woman and her brother as the true criminals.   Their manner, and much that they said in evidence, had seemed to favour this belief, nevertheless the accused had been condemned.   Would he speak, or would he take upon himself the guilt of others and die in silence ?

'Whatever he does, it is dreadful!' said Polly, shuddering.

'Still the person who committed the murder

is the one who ought to die,' said Miss Everilda, with a very unusual appreciation of the logical bearings of the question.

' It is so terrible to take the life of any one,' said Polly. ' What a state he must be in, and the judge and the barristers must be miserable too.'

' Possibly they may be, but they have no time to indulge in feelings of that kind. They are in the court all day, and dine out every evening. Alnminster may not be a hospitable place, but it never fails to entertain the judges and barristers magnificently. People must dine, but I do wish they would not have balls on these occasions,' remarked Mr. Simonds.

' Ah! you are thinking of the Sheriff's ball in the beginning of next week ?' said Miss Everilda.

' Yes, and it is to be held in the Town Hall this time, and that wretched man in the condemned cell will be almost within hearing of the carriages and music.'

' Not really ?' asked Miss Everilda, with a

shudder, and then she looked distressfully at Polly. Polly had been straining every nerve to get a really pretty fancy dress to wear at that ball, which was one given by the High Sheriff to the town and county. 'It does seem unfeeling to dance at such a time!' said the elder lady, thoughtfully. 'I don't wonder that you disapprove of it, Mr. Simonds.'

'Oh, I don't want to express such a very strong opinion as that,' he answered. 'A gay ball-room is a terribly strong contrast to the interior of a condemned cell, and the two things will lie near together, that's all.'

'That is a great deal,' said Miss Everilda ; 'the contrast is awful. And yet, think what you will of us, Mr. Simonds, my dear little cousin and I were intending to go ; but I am not sure that we can do it now that you have made us realise what it would be.'

Polly sighed. She had so wished to go. She had never been to a costume-ball, never been to a good ball of any kind, and as Zeph had promised to send her a pretty dress from the Castle, it seemed as easy to go as delightful. Was she about to be deprived of this great pleasure? She was very sorry about that poor man in the prison, but a ball is always a ball. She looked at Miss Everilda. Miss Everilda was evidently thinking. At last she said, 'Mary, my love, I don't believe I can go.'

John watched Polly's anxious face, and wished he had held his tongue. What was he that he should prescribe to others what they should feel? He wished he had not been so stupid. 'I entreat you not to let anything that I have said make you change your mind,' said he, in great dismay. 'I would not for the world be the means of losing Miss Polly this pleasure. Why should she not dance? I spoke without much thought; after all, this man had no objection to go a great part of the way in the direction of murder, he admitted that he had a struggle with the unfortunate victim, and perhaps he actually was the murderer; the world cannot stand still because a murderer meets with his deserts.'

'Mr. Simonds, you are not saying quite what you think. If we do take a wretched criminal's life we should do it in sadness and sorrow, his crime points to some fault in us or our ancestors. Besides, if I did go I should be haunted by the thought of that cell. Dancing would seem miserably out of place. You agree with me, Mary, don't you, dear?'

Polly looked very grave. A great joy was surely slipping away from her, and she knew it.

'I cannot say I do not wish to go to the ball, cousin,' she replied, 'I am afraid I do; but I will give it up cheerfully if you wish it.' And Polly looked anxiously in Miss Everilda's face, waiting for her fate.

'I do, dear. I am not the kind of person who could go to a ball with any pleasure under such circumstances, and I——'

'If you please, ma'am, Jonathan Graham is at the door, and he says that generally about this time you do a little for him,' said a servant who had come in almost unheard.

'What does he want doing for him, Robert?' asked Miss Everilda.

'Please, ma'am, he will leave it to you, I think,' said Robert.

'Then take him five shillings,' said Miss Everilda ; 'that's what my dear father always used to give him. Is that not the best thing I can do, Mr. Simonds?'

John took a bold resolution.

'If you ask me,' said he, 'I really think it would be better to see him and learn what it will be best to do for him. It is seldom good to give money.'

'Isn't it? And I do seem to give so much.'

He was very anxious to have a word or two with Polly, and wanted Miss Everilda to leave them alone awhile. Miss Everilda slowly left the room, taking the precaution to have five shillings ready in her pocket, for she knew that it would end in her having to give it, however prudently she might resolve to act.

'My dear Polly,' said John Simonds, hastily,

' will you ever forgive me for what I have done? I am so sorry. I had not the least idea that Miss Everilda would take any of my words to heart and act on them so promptly.'

' It is disappointing,' said Polly, making no effort to hide her feelings. ' Perhaps I ought not to wish to go. There is a great deal of truth in what you said.'

' I ought to have been wise enough to hold my tongue.'

' No, not if you felt strongly on the point.'

' I did—I do ; but I cannot bear to think that I have lost you a pleasure. But have you really lost it?   I will speak to Miss Everilda.'

' You had better not. Besides, after what you have said, perhaps I should feel that I was doing something wrong.'

' Oh, no.   I must speak to her—I will.'

' But don't urge it if she seems to have made up her mind to stay away. I should not like you to do that, for she feels strongly when she does take up an idea.'

' But you?' said he, inquiringly.

'I? Oh, I am not to be pitied. You don't know how kind she is to me.'

Miss Everilda soon returned.

'I have had to give him ten shillings, poor fellow,' she exclaimed cheerily. 'He did not seem to think he could make five do this time.'

Then there was a short silence. John was wondering how best to prefer his request, and Polly waiting to hear it, but not in hope, for she knew that Miss Everilda would not go to the ball when once her feelings had been enlisted in favour of an opposite course. John was very much pleased with the way in which Polly had behaved. It was so entirely honest. She made no pretence of professing fine feelings if they were absent from her mind. She frankly said she should very much like to go, but was prepared to submit quietly if Miss Everilda persisted in staying away. He made an attempt to undo what he had done, but all in vain. A matter of sentiment was with Miss Everilda a matter of principle, and she could not be moved.

'After Mary's disappointment, my only regret is that I shall not see that dress,' she said, for she knew nothing of John's attachment to her other cousin. 'I should have liked to see her wear it. You don't know about that dress, Mr. Simonds, but I will tell you.'

'Oh, don't tell about it now,' said Polly, anxiously. 'I beg you not.'

'Oh yes, I must. Of course you know all about my eldest cousin——?'

'Tell it another time,' pleaded Polly, not knowing how to spare John the hearing of what would trouble him so much.

'I will tell it now, dear; why not? Mr. Simonds, I was going to say that of course you know all about my niece Josephine's marriage. She has married a man who is perfectly delightful, and he is the handsomest man I ever saw.'

John did not seem to be warmly interested, but there was no stopping Miss Everilda. She would tell all about Phillis Arnold, and how Zeph had worn the very dress that Sir Joshua had painted her in, and Mr. Daylesford had fallen in love with her there and then, and she had promised to lend her sister that self-same dress for the High Sheriff's ball.

John listened calmly. Polly looked at him from time to time and marvelled at it. Then he said, 'Miss Everilda, such a good idea has come into my head.'

'For a poem?' Miss Everilda asked eagerly.

'Oh no, for a ball. You have beautiful rooms, do give one here—a fancy-dress ball, and let me come and see Miss Polly in the dress you have just told me about.'

Polly drew a long breath of joy. Joy because of the chance of this ball, and also because John seemed able to hear about Zeph without so much anguish as of old. He had indeed shown no sign of anguish at all, and he was even willing to see that dress.

'I'll think about it,' said Miss Everilda; and then Polly knew that the thing was done.

'You had better write by this post to tell

Zeph you don't want her to send the dress yet,' said Miss Everilda. ' Even if I did give a ball here, we had better not have it sent till just before the time when it is wanted. It is a very handsome dress, trimmed with valuable pearls, and it is always kept at Berkhampstead Castle,' she added, turning to John to explain her anxiety.

Polly did so wish her cousin would leave Zeph, and the Daylesford jewels, and Berkhampstead Castle, and all that Zeph had sold herself for, out of her conversation when John was present. Secrecy as to love affairs may be commendable, but it often causes pain and embarrassment.

Miss Everilda was never left in peace for long. Robert reappeared. ' If you please, ma'am, Widow Jackson's youngest boy has come running to say that the old linen has never got there, and that the doctor was very particular about the bandage being changed to-day. And please, ma'am, he says that the doctor did go on so last time because it had not stayed on well, and he said it ought to be a figure-of-eight bandage.'

Miss Everilda put her hands to her ears and said impatiently, ' These people are the plague of my life ! What is a figure-of-eight bandage ? It is no use coming to me, Robert, about such things as that. I never did understand figures, and I never shall.'

' I'll go to the Jacksons', cousin ; it is not a mile off. Let me go and see what they mean, and then I can try to do it, and I can take the old linen at the same time,' said Polly.

' Oh, will you really ? ' ejaculated Miss Everilda, much relieved. ' I shall be so much obliged to you, dear. I'll tell you what I will do, darling ; if you will do this for me I'll write to Zeph about the dress for you, and then I will take a large sheet of paper and make a list of all the nice people I know. I will not have any who are not nice. And then we will write and ask them to our ball.'

' And I will walk to the Jacksons' with you, Polly, if you will allow me ? ' said John.

' Thank you,' she replied ; and they went.

' And now I hope you will forgive me,' said he. ' Your cousin will give a delightful ball, and when we go back we will both set to work to write the invitations from her list.'

' My dear John,' exclaimed Polly, 'how little you know my cousin. When we go back she will have made no list. Do you think if she has a large sheet of blank paper spread before her, she will write anything on it but a poem ? '

CHAPTER XXIV.

PARIS BORDONE.

Mess. But yet, madam.
Cleo. I do not like *but yet*, it does alloy
The good precedence, fie upon *but yet.—Antony and Cleopatra.*

Fair and of all beloved, I was not fearful
Bluntly to give my life into your hand,
And at one hazard all my earthly means.—HEYWOOD.

MAY, June, and a large part of July had come and gone, and Zeph was gradually becoming part of the great world. The men whom her husband had always known brought their mothers, wives, and sisters to call on their friend's wife—he had 'ranged' himself, and the past was buried deep and well. At one time Zeph had told herself that she should never be happy in that house now that she had been brought face to face with its former history; and for days and even weeks she had gone about looking outwardly calm and contented, but with a heart full of scornful bitterness. Latterly she had attained to a quiet feeling of resignation—such wicked things were —Godfrey was no worse than many others; he loved her truly now, and was not likely to change. He was very good and kind, and had shared all he had with her. She knew that she did not love him as he loved her—that she had always known; but she felt very grateful and affectionate to him, and believed that, as time passed by, this feeling would, if anything, strengthen. Meantime the life she lived was entirely to her taste. It was a life of gay and pleasant luncheons and dinners, balls, theatres, and concerts. She need never spend an evening at home unless she wished. Her husband made her a liberal allowance, and she knew that if she exceeded it he would not complain. She indulged therefore freely in her taste for pretty dresses, and was admired wherever she went. Sometimes she said, ' Is not this a sweet dress, Godfrey ? '

'Ah, my darling,' he replied, 'it is pretty; but you looked just as charming in the simple little dresses you wore when I first knew you.'

'Oh, they were terrible!' said she, feeling a pang at the very recollection of them. 'What a dreadful time that was! I never had anything I wanted.'

'Say that you are happier with me,' pleaded Daylesford. She was not demonstrative enough for him, and he often longed to hear some spontaneous expression of affection from her.

'Happy! Of course I am happy,' she answered on one of these occasions; 'I am leading just the life I like best.'

'But would you be happy with me if we were poor and living in a little cottage in the country? I should be happy anywhere; but would you?'

'Oh, don't talk about things that are never likely to happen,' she answered evasively. 'I am afraid I should want some dancing even in the country, and what should I do when I wanted a new dress?'

Daylesford was so honest and straightforward, and so in love with her, that though he would have liked a loving declaration that she could be happy anywhere so long as he was with her, he never doubted her affection. 'You would have to rely on my ingenuity to help you,' said he ; 'I once did find a dress for you.'

'You did ; and by the way, Godfrey dear, I have promised it to Polly. She is to stay a fortnight longer at Seaton Court with my cousin Everilda, to go to a costume-ball at Alnminster. The High Sheriff is going to give it to the judges, or the judges are going to give it in honour of the High Sheriff, I forget which way it is, but it is no matter, only poor Polly had not an idea what to wear till I said she might have that old dress I wore—the loan of it, I mean.'

Daylesford looked perplexed. 'I wish ——' said he, and stopped.

'You wish what, dear?   Let me hear what it is.'

'I wish you had not said that your sister might have that dress—I don't think she can have it. It is not mine. It is part and parcel of the heirlooms at Berkhampstead, and it cannot be worn to look well without the lace and jewels belonging to it. Those things are all Marmaduke's, and though I did not mind your wearing them when you were staying in the house, I cannot consent to bring them away and send them to Alnminster. It would seem as if I looked on them as my own ; if you were going to wear them it would be different.'

' Let it be different as it is. You can easily give the order to Mrs. Sanderson to let us have them as you did before.'

' Of course I can ; but do forgive me if I say I don't like to do it.'

' I am sure Marmaduke would not mind.'

' I know he would not, but I do. The circumstances of the case oblige me to be so much more particular. Go to your dress-maker or to a costumier, and order Polly the prettiest dress you can design—it shall be my present to her.   I should like to make her a present.'

Zeph was dissatisfied. 'It is immensely kind of you, dear, but when you have a dress already which is just the very thing, why not let her wear it and save all trouble and expense?'

'But I haven't a dress!' said Daylesford. 'My dear Zeph, it seems a trifle to you to borrow it, and it is a trifle; but I do want to be very scrupulous in all my dealings with Marmaduke's property.'

'I will write and tell him about it,' said Zeph; 'and suppose I ask him to give me leave to use one of the family dresses sometimes if I want one for a ball?'

'You must do nothing of the kind, Zeph; it would only remind him of a thoroughly disagreeable and painful subject. He would write back and say that I have more right to settle what is to be done with everything at the Castle than he, and that in any case he will hand over all the dresses and jewels to you. Dear Zeph, leave things at the Castle alone. I understand Marmaduke better than you do. You would pain him terribly.'

'I don't want to pain him or you either.'

'Of course you don't. Go and get the people who understand these things to make your sister a beautiful dress. I will go with you, and then I shall see that you order a handsome one. Stop, I have an idea. Polly is a good-looking girl; go to the National Gallery and choose a dress from one of the pictures, and then tell your dressmaker to make one like it. I'd have a Paris Bordone if I were you.'

' But I don't think we should have time for that. There would be so much writing backwards and forwards before everything was settled, that the dress would never reach Polly in time.'

' Don't write backwards and forwards; go and see about it yourself.'

'Go to Paris!' said Zeph, aghast at the idea.

'My dearest Zeph——' began Daylesford, in a tone of suppressed amusement, but he was afraid she would be humiliated if he pointed out her mistake.

'What is it?' she inquired; 'you did say Paris.'

'Yes, Paris Bordone, that's the name of a painter. Let us go and see if you like that picture of his I am thinking of as much as I do. It is a portrait of a Genoese lady in a magnificent crimson dress. Her hair is just like Polly's, and I am sure Polly would look well in her dress.'

'I am very ignorant, I fear,' said Zeph, humbly.

He began to fear it too. Books such as it would have been well for her to read had not formed part of her father's library. Daylesford resolved to devote himself to making her familiar with the subjects which no woman's mind should be without. That very morning he would take her to the National Gallery, and when they passed a bookseller's shop he would alight and buy her a copy of Browning's 'Poems.' Some one had lately asked her in his hearing if she did not think Browning's 'Men and Women' very fine, and she had inquired where they were to be seen? Finally she had been obliged to own that she had never heard either of the poet or the poems.

'Come,' said Daylesford, 'let us go.'

'My dear Godfrey,' she replied, 'I am so sorry about this. I am giving you such a great deal of trouble.'

'No, I like going to the National Gallery, and even if I didn't, I should like going with you.'

He got out and bought her the Poems on the way, but when he gave them to her she said, 'You need not have bought those books, dear; they are in the house already in one of the bookcases upstairs.'

He actually blushed. 'I forget what there is in those bookcases,' said he.

She looked sorrowfully in his face, for she

was afraid she knew why he never stopped to look at those books.

They chose the picture he had in his mind—the yellow-haired lady with the rich crimson dress. 'We must send your sister a photograph of it, and then she will know how she ought to look,' said Daylesford.

'Thank you ; you think of everything,' said Zeph. 'My dressmaker can make a dress like that quite easily, and Polly will look very well in it. Now let us go.'

'Go!' he repeated ; 'not yet. Wait a minute or two longer. I don't suppose you have been often here.' He was shocked with himself for having said this ; the thought had passed through his mind, but the words had escaped him unawares.

It did not seem to strike her as one of those things which are best left unsaid. She answered quite calmly, 'I? Oh, hardly ever. In fact, I believe, only once.'

'But, my darling, you ought to know these pictures well. Some of them are magnificent.

We have one of the finest galleries in Europe. It is a delight to see such pictures as these. You feel that, I am sure, but if you didn't I should still have to make you study them. It is absolutely necessary to do so as a part of education. You can scarcely spend an evening in the society of people of any cultivation without being tripped up by your ignorance if you are not familiar with them.' They walked slowly round some of the rooms, Daylesford, who had a genuine love of art, pointing out picture after picture for her admiration as they went. She was meantime secretly meditating on the fact that after all she was by no means so well equipped for society as she had believed herself to be. Something more was wanted than youth, beauty, good means, liveliness of manner, and fair wits. More than once lately she had been convicted of gross ignorance on points on which it was vital to be well informed. If she had made that lamentable blunder about Paris Bordone, in society, society would have mocked her; it would have been whispered about as a good joke whenever she was seen or named, and whithersoever she went she would have been conscious of a tell-tale twinkle in the eyes of people around her which would reveal the fact that they knew and enjoyed a good story against her. How dreadful! And then if she said more things of this kind, Godfrey would at last be disgraced by having a wife whom it seemed legitimate to point out as the maker of all the malaprops and blunders that float about on the surface of society's small-talk and constitute so much of its joy. 'Very beautiful, dear, very finely painted, I should imagine,' she said with her tongue, but her mind was entirely given to these thoughts. How many of these ignorant and laughable speeches had she already made without being aware of them? Perhaps she was already beginning to be regarded as a person destined to afford society a liberal share of amusement. Godfrey had witnessed her want of knowledge when a great living poet and his works had been named, and that was why he had bought her

those books. He had just told her that she
would be considered woefully ill-educated if
she did not make herself acquainted with the
great pictures in this Gallery, and now he was
labouring hard to drive some knowledge of
them into her head. 'It is wonderfully fine,
dear,' she always said when he bade her admire
one, but with so many important things to
think about as she had, she could not give him
her full attention. Did that other person know
all these pictures by heart? Was she thoroughly familiar with all that was good in
literature and art? Was she, perhaps, wicked
though she was, well-educated and intellectual,
and therefore, so far as companionship was concerned, superior to Zeph herself? Zeph felt
her heartstrings tightening as this thought came
to torment her, but she did not, could not, and
would not believe it.

'Where does one get to know all about
these painters?' said she, after a determined
effort to profit by her opportunities and enjoy
his guidance round the rooms. He named some

books, but told her that the pictures themselves were the things to study, not the lives of the painters or what men wrote about them and their work ; that people could find out far more about a painter's character from his work than in any amount of books.

'Godfrey,' said Zeph once more, 'I never knew how very little I had learnt or been taught till I got to know you. Will you make me learn things and teach me as much as you can? It would be a dreadful thing if ever you were ashamed of me.'

'I am ashamed of you now,' said he, tenderly. 'How can you say such a thing as that in a public place like this, when you know that I can't take you to my heart and tell you that you are my own, and that I shall never have any feeling for you but true love?'

Zeph raised her dewy eyes from the floor and looked comforted and pleased, and she did not attempt to hurry him away from the pictures, though she was longing to get to her dressmaker's. That pleasure was hers in time, and Daylesford went with her, and between them they chose a really beautiful dress for Polly, and then Daylesford was dropped at his club and Zeph went home. As soon as she was alone she fell a-thinking of the alarming discovery she had made of her want of education. She had never before known that education was of so much importance. She had already been mortified to see how much her husband had felt her deficiency. He always looked so surprised when she did not seem to know things. Had he always been acquainted with women who were thoroughly on a level with his expectations? Had that other person whose name she had never heard, but who now occupied more of her thoughts than she liked, been more fitted for society than she herself was? Such an idea was inconceivably bitter to Zeph—to know that it was true would cut her to the heart.

Some fascination of which she could render no account made her at once go upstairs to that lovely sitting-room which as yet she had

never been able to use as her own. It seemed
intended for her, but she had never been able
to feel happy in it, and she had remarked that
her husband had never once said, 'Why don't
you sometimes sit in that room upstairs?' To-
day she went to it without pausing for a
moment, and at once began to examine the
books. First she carefully read their titles. If
her knowledge of such matters had not been so
limited, she would have seen that all the
greatest poets of England, France, and Germany
were represented on those shelves, and that
most of the masterpieces of English prose
literature had found a place in the second
white bookcase. Zeph thought that some of
these masterpieces must be very dull if their
titles were to be trusted, but for the present
left that point undetermined. What she next
did was to take out each book, one after the
other, to see if any name—any woman's name.
—were written on the blank pages. Her reason
told her that it was impossible that this should
be the case, that Godfrey himself would have

seen to the removal of anything that might give her pain, but in spite of reason she had a haunting dread of what she might perchance discover. Her task was a long one, but no such name appeared. Once or twice she found Daylesford's—never any other—and the sense of relief she experienced was immense. Then she went to the writing-table and opened all the drawers. There were a number of them, but all were empty; there was not a bit of ribbon, a scrap of paper, or anything. All were daintily lined with clean white paper and ready to receive anything that she herself chose to put into them. Whatsoever this room had once held that had belonged to another was to all appearance gone; it was now swept and garnished for herself. Could she bring herself to use it? It only required one plunge and the thing would be done. Why should she not occupy it? Why should any sentiment either of regret or repugnance be allowed to cling for ever about this one room? She went into her own room and brought some embroidery she was busy with, and spread it out and scattered her silks about on one of the tables. She cut open the books Godfrey had just given her, and left them lying on the sofa ; then she went to the bookcase to seek a book, for she was going to work in earnest, she was about to try to cultivate the waste and desolate places of her mind. It was a gigantic task, and the sooner she took it in hand the better. She found a French book ; French had of late often been her despair. She could read easy conversations, or thought she could, for the difficulties in French are so subtle that they usually evade the sight of ignorant persons, but a bit of description was to her an impenetrable jungle. She began to read with a firm purpose of looking out in the dictionary every word that she did not know ; Godfrey should not be ashamed of her, she would not be ashamed of herself. She had never done any work of this kind, and found it very irksome, but she performed her task for nearly an hour with complete fidelity. Then she began to wish that Godfrey would return home, or some one amusing come to call. Why did not Agnes come more frequently, and she wanted to see Jack? While she was wondering if she had time to go and see them, a letter was brought to her. It was from Miss Everilda. ' I write, my dear Zeph, to ask you not to send the dress. Mary and I have given up all idea of attending the High Sheriff's ball. I am ashamed I ever had such an idea. It is strange what even high-minded women will do if they look at things one-sidedly. We looked at this on the side of our amusement, but a dear young friend who often spends some of his leisure hours with us——' ' *His* leisure,' thought Zeph with a weight of lead on her heart already, ' and hours too ! '—— ' has persuaded us not to go. He wants me to give a fancy-dress ball at Seaton Court, to make up to your sister for this disappointment. I am afraid she is disappointed, though she has taken it so sweetly, dear girl. I think I shall adopt his suggestion. I like doing what he wishes, and besides that I think I should enjoy seeing this handsome old house looking once more like itself. Therefore, dear Zeph, though I ask you not to send the dress now, please send it a little later, for I should dearly like to see Mary wear it in my house. And now I must say good-bye, for they have gone for a long walk together, and I want to have my list of the people who ought to be invited, ready for them when they come back. I believe you knew something of Mr. Simonds before you were married, at least I think he told me about an hour ago that he had some acquaintance with you, but I will ask him again. Yours ever, Everilda.'

Zeph folded her hands and laid her head down on the table on them. She had never thought of this happening. Why should Polly, who was young, handsome, and free—why should Polly, who had the whole world before her to choose from, choose this one man? Zeph had sometimes thought it would be an almost unbearable pain to her if he married any one, but if he married her own sister it would be a thousand times worse. And yet he had a right to marry any one he chose; the tie between herself and him was broken. The worst of it was that she had never quite felt that it was broken—stupid, irrational, wicked, mad, let any one call it what they chose—so long as he was unmarried he still seemed to belong to her more than to any one, and she could sometimes even think of him with a quiet regard and love in which as she believed there was no sin. If he married Polly she must never think of him in that way again; she must never see him, of course. She had, however, never intended to see him again. She could live as she was living now with Daylesford in the bonds of quiet affection, and could go on living with him for ever happily enough, if John did but keep out of her way. She did not believe she should ever be able to meet him unmoved. Even if she never saw him till she was quite an old woman she feared that her heart would blaze up with love for the man whom she had treated so ill. No tear passed the barrier of her eyelids—tears were impossible ; the heart wound she was suffering from lay far too deep down for any tears to rise to her eyes—far too deep for her to visit it save on very rare occasions.   She sat where she was for more than an hour, and was roused at last by a kind hand on her shoulder.

'Why, Zeph, my darling, what are you doing?'   Daylesford was the speaker.   He saw the French book and the open dictionary, but he almost thought his wife had been asleep. 'Were you asleep?   Have I disturbed you?'

Zeph raised her head, which really did look half stupefied with sleep, and said, 'Asleep, oh no, I don't think I have been asleep; I am sure I have not.'

'Of course you have,' said he ; 'you would not deny it so fervently if you had not.   Let me have a look at you.'   He had not seen the face he loved so much for some hours.

She looked up, but could not meet his eyes : they were full of such honest, generous, and true affection, that she shrank away from the sight of them—she was so utterly unworthy of it. He was too good himself to suspect any shortcoming, not to mention disloyalty, in any one without absolute proof, much less in her. He had no conception what thoughts had been passing through her mind, and only said, ‘ I wish I had let you sleep a little longer, dear.’

His kindness touched her to the heart—it always had done so. Never must she give way to such thoughts again ; it was foolish, it was wicked, it was treacherous in the highest degree to him whom she had vowed to love, and whom, please God, she would end by loving—if she did not, it should not be for want of trying. Not for worlds would she ever let Godfrey suspect any part of what had been passing through her mind while she had been alone. ‘ I have had a tiring day,’ said she. ‘ To begin with, we went out, you know, and then after I came home I did all kinds of things before I sat down to read some French.’

‘ French ! ’ he exclaimed ; he had never seen her open a French book since they were married.

'Godfrey,' she said, very humbly, 'I am so anxious to improve myself a little, I can't bear being so ignorant as I am. I have been trying to learn a little by myself, but I think you must let me have some lessons.'

END OF THE SECOND VOLUME.

PRINTED BY
SPOTTISWOODE AND CO., NEW-STREET SQUARE
LONDON